# The Dignity of Danger

# THE DIGNITY OF DANGER

## A Novel of the Pacific War

## Everard Meade

*"The profession of soldiers and sailors has the dignity of danger."*
Samuel Johnson

BURNING GATE PRESS
LOS ANGELES

For information address:
Burning Gate Press
P. O. Box 6015
Mission Hills, CA 91395-1015
(818) 896-8780

FIRST EDITION

Library of Congress Catalog Card Number: 92-75973

ISBN 1-878179-09-8

To the men of the aircraft carrier *Franklin*

This book is dedicated to *Franklin's* officers and men, living or dead. Survivors will realize that this is not really their story; there are some parallels, but there are obvious differences, the dates, for example.

I've never forgotten the Spring day in 1945 when *Franklin* sailed into Pearl Harbor, completing an incredible sea voyage from the Philippine Islands while still carrying heavy battle damage. It was a peaceful morning with the westerlies shaking palm fronds and making little waves in the channel off Ford Island. Carriers coming into port customarily turn out their crew in whites all around the flight deck. *Franklin's* crew were lined up from the island aft–silent evidence that she had lost a third of her people. Her whole forward section was a mass of rusty, twisted steel beams and ripped-up decking with the forward elevator gone and part of the bridge smashed. Even her band, playing "Anchors Aweigh," sounded a bit ragged. You lose that many men, no one is safe, not even a trumpet player.

When she was tied up, I joined a small crowd who went aboard looking for friends. Below deck the blackened passageways smelled of scorched paint, burnt wood, cordite, and gasoline–bitter odors, suggesting all too clearly what had happened there. Some visitors found their friends; others were not so lucky. What I found in the battered ship was an inspiration for a story of hardship and bravery.

"The enemy" had their share of both. No Pacific war story, fiction or real, would be complete without also acknowledging the bravery of the Japanese. The two tales, concurrently told, are imaginary.

## Acknowledgements

I am grateful to two senior U.S. naval aviators for technical and editorial assistance. They are Captain William D. Fries, USN (Ret) and Captain Walter C. Blattmann, USN (Ret).

For guidance and information about the Japanese armed forces, I have received much background help from *The Divine Wind* by Captain Inoguchi, *Thunder Gods* by Naito, and *The Japanese Navy In World War II*, published by the U.S. Naval Institute. Hoyt's *The kamikazes* was especially helpful. So was *Mission Beyond Darkness* by Lt. Commander J. Bryan III and Philip Reed.

I would also like to thank Captain Masanori Koga, JMSDF, assistant naval attaché at the Embassy of Japan in Washington, D.C. for critically examining the Japanese material.

The idea of including the Japanese viewpoint was contributed by my friend and agent, Dorris Halsey.

In this work of pure fiction an attempt has been made to imagine how a handful of combatants may have felt. Most stories are imaginary— as are most ships, people, and places. Only the dangers and the courage are consistently real.

—E.M.

*The Dignity of Danger*

# Part I

# One

*October, 1944*

The Admiral poked a slip of paper at me. It bore the coordinates our submarine had sent for the Japanese battleship. The Admiral expected me to locate the spot on his chart. With calipers I took the distances from the edge of the chart and "walked" them in. Easy enough, but with three stars standing behind me holding a yellow pin I found myself double-checking everything.

Normally a group's Air Combat Intelligence Officer doesn't find himself working for a vice admiral; the regular flag ACI had been returned to Pearl with ulcers. Studying the coordinates and calculating them with a prayer, I became aware of the Admiral's rough breathing as well as the creaking of the bulkhead. Finally, I made the interception and the Admiral pounced on the spot with his pin, as if I'd found a bug he'd sworn to exterminate.

We stood off the Philippine Islands. The sub had sighted the Japanese battleship east and south of our position. A massive confrontation gathered on both sides. With 270,000 men dug in ashore Japan divided her surface fleet into three major naval forces which would steam through the Philippine Straits to surprise and confuse the attacking Americans—a threat that worried our Admiral about as much as rumors of migrating whales.

"How far?" the Admiral asked, lighting a cigarette.

"Close to 300 miles," his Chief of Staff said, looking at me.

I nodded. I knew all of our aircraft were committed and felt sorry for the old man, who had found an unexpected target and had no aircraft to launch. Our carrier had become the task force flagship upon his arrival and—at his order—had sent off our entire air group toward a Philippine position.

Dan Duncan was embarked with us in *Sussex*, an *Essex*-class carrier with a flight deck as long as two football fields and an air group of 90 planes. Supporting them nearly 3,000 men pumped the gas, repaired bullet holes, fired the guns, loaded the ammo, chipped the rust, baked the bread and ran the semaphores. A complement of officers commanded the usual divisions, and a few officers—the ACIs—briefed and debriefed the fliers. In the fall of '44 you might say I was an ACI who'd been kicked upstairs.

The Pacific doesn't always live up to her name. In the heavy seas that day *Sussex* groaned like a schooner under sail. Her deck rose slowly, then tipped forward as plane handlers criss-crossed the teak surface in the rain, slanting figures leaning into the wind.

The Captain came clattering down from the main bridge, stepped in, and saluted, a small man with a brisk authoritative manner, dressed in freshly pressed khakis. "You sent for me, Admiral?" A faint hint of reproach.

The Admiral smiled and held out the coordinates. "You see this about the Jap heavy unit?"

The Captain took the paper and nodded.

The Admiral's smile widened. "Our sub says he got one of their cans."

The old man pointed to the chart where his pin had skewered the enemy. "Tempting target, McCord." A chess player moving the first pawn.

"Too bad we have no planes," McCord said. "Our entire group is headed for Pindoro."

This was hardly news to the old sailor. "Where are they?"

The Captain looked at his watch, then swung around to me. "Mike?"

"Halfway to the island, Captain." I closed the calipers and pointed. "About here."

"Too bad," McCord said, without much conviction.

The Admiral shot a stream of smoke tumbling against the rain-beaded glass.

"Suppose I asked you to bring 'em back? What would you say, Jim?"

I knew what this meant to McCord. Every fiber of his being would be resisting. He was first, last and always a Navy Regs officer who wouldn't dream of changing orders of an air group halfway to its target. Particularly, when the flight was part of a tactical plan ordered by the Supreme Allied Commander.

"I can't do it, Admiral. General MacArthur wouldn't..."

"Fuck General MacArthur," the Admiral said genially. "Nimitz sent me out here to clear the way for the landings and this looks like one way to do it." The Chief of Staff, a senior Navy captain named Stowell, removed his pipe and grinned.

McCord tried another tack. "We're armed for the island strike, Admiral. General purpose bombs. No armor piercing stuff aboard the aircraft. No APS. It'll take time to rearm."

"I know all that," the Admiral said gruffly. "I'm asking a simple question. Have you got the balls to call 'em back?"

McCord spoke in a stronger voice. "Let's be frank, sir. The Navy knows whether I've got balls or not." Every man on the bridge knew he'd won a Navy Cross at Midway. "This is not about balls, it's a question of responsibility. MacArthur expects our group to support what he's doing. He's looking to *Sussex* for cover and preliminary bombardment..."

The Admiral was not impressed. "You forget I was part of the formulation of this plan, McCord. The mighty General didn't just lift his corncob one day and dream up the whole thing out of blue smoke. The Navy was there."

McCord said nothing. "You're thinking this is a wild goose chase, Jim?" the old man said, in a reasonable voice.

"It's sure as hell a long shot, Admiral."

"Granted, but still a shot."

McCord took a step closer to the old man, looking up into the weathered face. "Not much of one, sir. Here's what we've got. The flight's been gone for ninety minutes. We call 'em back, add ninety minutes. Thirty, forty minutes to bring 'em aboard, if they're letter perfect which is rare. We get wave-offs, guys going into the barricades because the deck's wet. Ninety landings take time. Then you got rearming. A real bitch. Never saw them do it in less than an hour and a half. We just can't handle that armor-piercing stuff like footballs. Another thirty to take off and form up. A lot of time, Admiral."

The old man nodded. McCord continued, "That's three hours and a half minimum. At the moment it's just eleven hundred. Which means they start the second strike at fourteen-thirty. The sighting is three hundred miles away. Not allowing for him to move in our direction, that's two hours. Sixteen-thirty. If they find him, another half hour attack time. Then home, we'd have a night landing, sir. Bad news."

"Night landings aren't the end of the world, McCord. Your group has done 'em before. Every group certified for carrier duty has learned to come aboard in the dark. I've even done it myself."

"So have I," the Captain replied. "But I didn't like it. The Admiral is deliberately placing eighty or ninety pilots at risk."

The old man's jaw stuck out. "Risk is the name of the game, McCord. Nobody in this man's navy is free from it. My classmates aboard the

Arizona, asleep in their beds tied up to the fucking dock in the harbor, were about as safe as you could get. Talk about risk. Name of the game, my friend."

The Admiral walked over and opened the door to the wing of his bridge. The rain blew in as he stepped outside. We watched him out there alone making his decision. The bill of his cap made him look like a fisherman scanning the sea for marlin. His face was old leather, creased by a lifetime of squinting at sun on water. The sea rose in big swells, and a few frigate birds skimmed and dipped close to the surface like cross-country skiers. Below him the flight deck was bustling with activity. We could see plane handlers hurrying along, against the wind and rain. A yellow tractor pulled a blue Hellcat off the forward elevator, which then sank to the hangar deck with klaxons.

The old man put his back to the wind, and watched the plane guard destroyer nosing along 165 degrees off the stern, ready to fish out the strays if they had to ditch. Was he thinking "Tonight maybe?" On the port side, aft, Landing Signal Officers huddled together, instinctively glancing skyward, though nobody was due for hours.

I thought the Captain had done a pretty good job of shooting down the idea. While we were waiting, the Captain studied the chart. After about ten minutes, the Admiral returned, brushing the rain off his zippered jacket. His expression was grim as he went up to the Captain. "Let's bring 'em back, Jim. We've got to get this sucker if we can. That's what they're paying us for." McCord took a deep breath. He had done all he could do. Time to obey orders. "Aye, sir."

# Two

"What do we say to MacArthur?" McCord asked.

The Admiral, who had been looking grim, smiled and said, "We'll send him a 'You know dear.'"

"Jesus," McCord murmured.

"Why the hell not?" the Admiral said.

"Let's have a yeoman."

In less than five minutes a crewman with crossed quill pens on his sleeve seemed to appear out of nowhere. The Admiral put on his glasses and smiled at the tense yeoman who stood poised with pad ready to write.

"You know what a *you know dear* is, son?"

"Yes, Admiral. UNODIR. 'Unless otherwise directed.'"

The Admiral nodded. "This one goes to General MacArthur, Supreme Allied Headquarters, Philippines."

The yeoman's eyes rolled as his pen scribbled down words that meant this old man was pulling the *Sussex* planes out of the Philippine assault. Oh, brother!

But for a training accident that left me with a badly damaged right eye and no wings on my chest, I might have been out there with them. Actually, I was lucky to be on active duty as Air Combat Intelligence Officer—an assignment wangled through all sorts of Navy chicanery and twenty-six weeks of schooling at Quonset Point, Rhode Island. The more miraculous because it was accomplished over the objections of my wife, a small, lovely woman with two daughters and a firm conviction that I belonged at home.

Although I was assigned to the Admiral, it was my air group, so I went along with the Captain as he returned to the main bridge, above the Admiral's bridge, and made the recall, in a dry, impersonal voice, "Mako Sharks. This is mother. Return immediately. Repeat. Home to mother soon."

I could picture the pilots' reaction to such a message. Fritz, their CAG, would probably be too busy to wonder what came next. He had to make sure all his hot shots dropped their bombs in the water; you don't land on a carrier with your armament, and then formed up to return to base. Up ahead, half hidden in the mist, two cans plunged along, side by side, guarding against enemy subs.

The executive officer (XO) was Commander Barry Barker. Captain Mac was the boss, but Big Barry really ran most things. The crew had an affection for him, but they knew if they screwed up, he'd have their ass for breakfast. I was sharing a cup of coffee with Barry when a hesitant knock sounded on the bulkhead outside the curtain. "Come in!" Barker roared. A small wiry man pushed aside the curtain and stepped in, breathing hard. "At ease, Chief. Sit down. You know Lieutenant Mason."

"Yes, sir, thank you, sir."

Barker slid a pack of Luckies across the desk, past a silver-framed picture of a handsome woman proudly holding a tennis racket. The Chief pulled out a cigarette and accepted a light from the Exec's Zippo. The blue flame was steady in the brown fist with the Academy ring. "What's up, Commander?"

"Plenty. They found a Jap BB, and we're going after him."

The Chief looked pained. "With what? Nobody's home. The strike isn't back yet."

The Exec lit a fresh Lucky from the one he was smoking. "The Admiral ordered them back to reload."

"I'll be a frog-eyed sonofabitch! What'd the Captain say?"

"He said, 'Aye, aye, Admiral'."

"Don't he know what a ball-buster this is?"

"He knows, Chief. All he said was 'do it'."

"Brother, am I screwed!"

"Up to here. And if you don't have those APs and fish on deck ready to load when they land, it'll be up to your neck."

"But sir, you know goddamn well..."

"What I know goddamn well," the Exec said jovially, "is that it's *got* to be done. Get every hand you can find. Wake 'em up. Drag 'em out of the sack."

At the door the Chief turned, shaking his head. "I can't use anybody but my own people, sir. One screw-up and the whole fucking ship goes."

"Okay, use everybody off watch too. Tell 'em to get those fish ready for the torpeckers or I'll have theirs."

"Aye, XO."

Right on schedule the Chief of Staff, pipe in hand, said, "Here they come, Admiral."

"Great!" The old man checked his watch and he stepped out in the light rain, setting his cap with a tug on the bill. I watched him light a cigarette in cupped hands, back to the wind, and stash the match in the recessed ashtray. The sound of the returning planes grew stronger, a steady roar like waves breaking on a reef that changed in tone as they overflew.

I never got over the thrill of watching an air group come aboard. Below on deck, I could see the landing crew. The Landing Signal Officers with their paddles were in place on a platform, port side aft. The men on arresting cable waited for the plane's hook. The men at the crash barricade probably hoped to God they'd be out of work. The watch officer on the bridge of the destroyer would alert his swimmers in case of a ditching. On the hangar deck exhausted members of ordnance detail, pouring with sweat and naked to the waist, still positioned armor-piercing bombs and torpedoes, stacking them neatly and carefully for their massive reloading task.

In the first Hellcat Fritz Rawlings began a long dive that became a glide, slowing to ten knots above stalling speed and obeying the LSO's "little high." With full flaps he made a perfect touchdown and arrested landing. The Hellcat came to a quick stop, pulling the arresting cable into a deck-wide "V," then was jerked back a few feet by the donkey engine that rewinds the cable, allowing the Hellcat's hook to spit out the cable as Rawlings responded to a "hook up" signal and taxied forward to clear the deck for the next plane. Once clear of the landing area and parked, Fritz slid back his canopy and scrambled out, hurrying to find out why the flight had been recalled

I met Fritz in the ready room—a tall grinning man with high cheekbones and close-cut sandy hair. "Hey, Mike, what goes on?"

I offered him a cigarette.

"The Admiral has found a Jap battlewagon."

"Where?" he yelled, still a little deaf from the ear phones.

"Maybe 300 miles southeast."

"Holy shit. A battleship?"

I nodded. "He wants you to rearm and go get it."

He took a deep drag. "Heavy duty."

"Yep."

"Long day at the office."

"No doubt of it."

"I bet."

His Wingman, Terry Vernon, came lumbering down the passage and filled the room, or so it seemed. Terry really was too big to be a Navy flier but somehow he'd made it—for which Fritz Rawlings had long been grateful. Fritz handed him a cup of coffee. "Rest it, old man."

"Thanks. What's happening?" Terry had a pleasant North Carolina accent. "How come the recall?"

"A battleship." Fritz said. "A genuine Japanese battleship." The admiral wants us to go get it.

Terry took a loud sip. "I figured something important. Jesus. A battleship."

He was quiet for a moment, finishing his coffee. Then he turned to me, grinning. "Any news, Mike?"

"Not yet. No stateside cables. Mail call in a day or so."

"I wish she'd hurry."

"I wish so, too," Fritz said. "I want a wingman who can concentrate on keeping me alive."

Terry didn't find this amusing. "I'll always keep the monkeys off your back, Fritz. Don't you worry."

Fritz nodded, perhaps a little embarrassed that his wing man had taken him so literally. The rest of his group began to fill the room—with their smoke, their talk and laughing. I knew most of them by now, and with their squadron ACIs had sent them on their way that morning to their island target. Normally it would be my job to brief them on the new target, but I had word that the Admiral was coming. The room was stifling in spite of two rotary fans whose hum mingled with the subdued nervous chatter of a group waiting for the word. They all stood as the Admiral entered.

He waved them down and sat on the corner of a table, searching their faces with his pale blue eyes before speaking. He began with a grin. "Gentlemen, I apologize for screwing up your strike. In fact, I probably made naval history here today by calling off a mission ordered by General MacArthur."

They were too tense to laugh. This was big stuff and they were on edge.

The old man swung his arms forward, closed them across his flat stomach and lifted his chin. "Takes one helluva reason to do what I've done. Here it is: We've got a sighting on a Japanese task force headed this way—and we're going after them. Could be the biggest chance you'll ever have."

He was gratified to see their heads turn, their faces light up. His voice grew louder. "One battleship, gentlemen, two cruisers, and a bunch of cans. Target of a lifetime. You'll get the particulars from your ACI officers. I'm here to tell you why I brought you back and wish you luck."

They leaped to their feet again as he started to leave. He turned and said, "Sit down, boys." He probably shouldn't have called them that. But, that's all they were—and by sundown a lot of them could be gone.

Fritz took over, letting the Admiral's words do their work. Normally, Fritz's function as CAG was to give his fliers the order of battle. Other details—such as geographical data or fresh target information from photos—was generally added by the ACI. In the case of the Japanese battleship I had no new information, so he handled the whole briefing—like a master.

"Okay, fellas, this is it. If we can find this bugger, we've got ourselves, you heard the Admiral, 'the target of a lifetime.' As usual, the fighters will follow me in the primary attack, trying to chase the bastards from the deck guns. Drop your wing bombs, turn on your fifties, and sweep the fucking deck." He grinned and cleared his throat. "Dive bombers should aim for the bridge—or the stacks. Torpeckers come in low and be on the lookout for waterspouts from shells exploding in your path. And watch it, Jesse, don't be so fucking eager to come in too close that your fish doesn't get a chance to have an armoring run."

Stone had been talking to the other torpeckers in a low voice. "Sure, sure," he said, shifting uneasily in his chair. I was glad to see Fritz nail him.

When the briefing was over Fritz walked over to Jesse and said—in surprisingly pleasant tones—"Well, Jesse—this should be the target you've dreamed about."

Stone waved a tattered magazine with a nude girl on the cover. "Here's what I dream about. Not fucking battleships."

"You're lucky," Fritz said, picking up a cup of coffee. "If we can find 'em today, it's your chance to be a hero!"

"If you can find 'em."

Fritz took a sip. "Just wanted to say 'good luck, Jesse.'"

"You'll need the luck," Stone said, "finding the fuckers."

"Meaning?" Fritz's voice was cool.

"Ask your ACI friend here. He'll tell you how fucking far away this so called 'great target' is."

"I've studied the chart," Fritz said coldly.

"Then you know we can't go fucking around too fucking long without coming back in the dark."

"I'm aware of that factor."

"Bringing a group this size aboard in the dark is a bitch."

"Tell me about it, Jesse."

"Just be sure you don't waste too much time out there trying to please the Admiral."

"My job, Jesse, not yours—back off."

Frowning, Fritz walked out.

Terry Vernon, red in the face, stood towering over Jesse, who put down his magazine. "What's with you Vernon?"

"Plenty."

"So?" he said, raising an eyebrow.

"So who put the bug up your ass?"

"The hell are you talking about?"

"Rawlings is on our side. Remember?"

"Too fucking bad. The Japs can have him."

"Has he done something to you? Spit in your soup? Raped your sister?"

"I warned him for his own good. That's all."

"What makes you think he needs your help?"

"He's too fucking eager. Wants to look good for the old man. He'll kill us all before he's through. Typical of those bastards."

"Typical of—you mean regular Navy? You hate the Admiral, the Captain, the CAG. What did they ever do to you?"

"Bunch of pricks." In mountain accents this came out "preeucks."

I chimed in, "Don't talk like an idiot, Jesse. These men are professionals. Running the Navy is what they do. War or no war. We've only got one bunch of enemies—and they're not Fritz or the Captain or the Admiral."

"Don't preach to me, Mike Mason. What the hell do you know? Standing in the ready room and telling the boys where the target is and how much ack-ack we can expect, then you're up to the bridge with the fucking Captain and the fucking Admiral while the rest of us climb in our fucking planes and get the shit kicked out of us. Fuck off, Lieutenant. Just fuck off. When I need a sermon I'll go find a fucking preacher." He delivered this in a harsh voice with quick jabbing gestures; small eyes burning.

Like a man brushing off a fly, Terry said "Relax, old man. Save it for the Japs," and walked out.

I knew that Fritz liked to look in on his pilots when he had a chance and I helped him out as often as I could. As he saw me leave the ready room, he signaled for me to join him down the tilting passage. When a carrier turns into the wind in preparation for a launch (like now), the bow lifts in a way that makes walking difficult. Fritz pointed to a cubicle on my left. "Check on the kid for me will you, Mike?"

"Sure thing."

Fritz continued his slow progress down the creaking passage and I dropped in on young Senor Martinez. His tiny cubicle reminded me of a confessional in church. It wasn't much bigger and there was a rosary hanging from a small wooden cross above his bunk. A colored picture of Jesus was taped to the bulkhead. But I'm sure the smell of incense was my imagination.

"How's it going, Marty?"

"Okay, sir. *Bueno bueno*, as my father would say."

"Some of the guys are a little tense."

"Why not?" He forced a thin smile. "I'm not exactly loose, myself."

"That's natural."

"This is the big one—right?" He managed to broaden the smile.

"Right, Marty."

I could feel his tension, which belied his cheerful words. He looked down at the deck, then rolled his eyes to the overhead.

"You feel okay, Marty?"

"Maybe a little queasy, sir. It's always like this when we're heading into the wind. At home we call it *Mareo.*"

"I know what you mean, Marty. You'll be all right when you get airborne."

"Right. Absolutely, sir. Fit as a fiddle when I'm airborne."

"Yeah, sure."

I realized that he was going to tough it out. The one thing he wasn't going to do was admit he'd rather stay aboard. I gave him an encouraging pat and moved on. I was betting that rosary was about to take a trip.

# Three

"Lieutenant Mason to flag plot."

I found the Admiral bending over a chart with his Chief of Staff. The old man wore silver spectacles, which made him look more like a professor than a sailor.

"Another sighting, Mike." He held out a slip of paper.

With more assurance this time I repeated the calipers procedure. Where my two lines crossed the Admiral stuck another pin. He leaned over and squinted at it, then touched the first pin.

"Moving this way."

"Looks like it," Chief of Staff said. "Relative bearing of 95 degrees."

The Admiral yanked off his glasses and slowly twirled them in his right hand. For a moment the only sounds in the plot room were from outside, the dot-dashes from the radio shack, the klaxon of the forward elevator, a bosun's whistle, followed by "Now hear this..."

The Admiral cleared his throat. "I wish he'd hurry."

Anticipating his next question, I took the dividers and worked out the Japanese position. "He's making 18 knots, sir."

The Admiral nodded. "So two hours is 36 miles closer." Turning to me, he said, "Get this to Rawlings."

"Aye, sir." I grabbed the paper and took off.

I found Fritz on the hangar deck chatting with his crew chief, a cocky little New Yorker named Joe Panetta. The air was full of whining steel-on-steel sounds, and smelled high of gasoline and oil. Joe greeted me with Italian charm. "Ciao, Mr. Mason. You come down to see if the CAG knows where the hell he's going?"

"You got it, Joe."

Leaning out of the cockpit, Fritz shouted, "What's going on?"

I waved the dispatch. "Admiral's got a new target for you." I climbed a ladder and gave him the slip of paper.

His eyebrows went up. "Looks like the Japs are coming to meet us."

"Looks like it."

"It's still one helluva long run. What do you figure?"

"Over 300 nautical miles. Not exactly a stroll in the park."

"Not exactly."

Fritz, starting down the ladder, called out, "Maybe I should take you along, Joe. Give you something to talk about."

"In a pig's ass you will. I got plenty to talk about already. Watch the fucking oil pressure on this baby, Commander. I don't like what I see."

"Will she get me there and back? That's all I ask."

"That she'll do. I don't guarantee what a few bullet holes will do. Stay away from the fucking machine guns and you'll be fine."

"Thanks, Joe. Am I sound and ready?"

Joe slapped the huge blue fighter affectionately. "She's ready, sir. Don't know about you."

Fritz grinned. "I'm ready. Mike?"

"I've got the new charts. Your place?" I said.

"Okay. Thanks, Joe."

"Sure. Sure. Give 'em hell, Fritz." He roared with laughter at his own audacity.

After a brief meeting with Fritz I returned to flag plot. The Admiral asked if Fritz had the sighting and I said, "Yes."

The Admiral opened the door to the wing of the bridge, suddenly admitting the ear-splitting roar of the warm-up, and stepped out in the light rain. The flight deck was a scene of regulated chaos—a dangerous place where a careless crewman can get himself killed amid steel propellers spinning at 800 revolutions per minute.

Nobody among the plane handlers liked to recall what happened off San Diego when they were learning their jobs. I remembered the big likable clumsy fellow with a Slavic name ending in "iski". He had backed into a Hellcat prop and few people could eat their dinner that night after they swabbed the deck. The accident had spawned a cruel watchword. Don't be an "iski"—meaning, "Watch where the hell you're going on the flight deck or you'll get your head cut off."

The fighters stood first in line, awaiting deck take-off. They were spotted tail-to-prop, whipping the rain into silver discs and scouring the wooden deck with prop wash. Clipped to their wings were six rockets ready to discourage anti-aircraft gunners and soften the way for the dive bombers, who were spotted next, armed with APs. Back of the bombers the torpeckers were underbellied with fish that could sink a battleship.

The Admiral watched the young pilots stream out of the island and jog toward their aircraft. Some emerged singly, heading down against the wind; others came out in pairs, yelling at each other, occasionally slapping a shoulder for good luck as they threaded their way among the spotted planes. How he must have longed to be with them, leading a dive or carrying a torpedo! He turned to his Chief of Staff, raising his voice. "What time did we say the sun goes down?"

"A little after nineteen-hundred, sir."

The Admiral looked at his wristwatch. "Going to be close." He looked at the sky. "Dark comes so fast out here."

"Yes, sir."

The rest was left unspoken as the crew spotted the leading Hellcat for its deck run. All eyes turned to the big blue fighter with Rawlings in the cockpit. He raised his hand in a thumbs-up gesture and pushed the Hellcat down the forward deck at high speed while the crewmen cheered. Fritz Rawlings cleared the bow and climbed sharply, waiting for his men to join up.

I knew that a surge of excitement must be coursing through Fritz, a special tingling that always came in the presence of danger. You could spend a lifetime in the Navy and never have a shot at a battleship. After a little trouble with binoculars, I managed to see that Terry Vernon had formed up and the rest of the squadrons were rising in good shape. Soon the whole flight looked no bigger than a bunch of migrating geese going east on a bearing of 95 degrees.

As I watched them disappear, I sent up a prayer. Eighty-five kids heading into combat with what kind of unspoken fears in their hearts? Of course, there were some genuine tigers who couldn't wait to find the monster target. And there must be others who sweated a little when they thought of finding the great battleship and diving into her bristling defenses. No doubt Fritz would be in the tiger group. His courage had been proven at Midway and on the Coral Sea. Terry had been there covering his tail. And there'd be Jesse Stone with ice in his veins. Jesse, the coal miner's son, a man to reckon with whether you were American or Japanese.

All day I had been hopping around the ship, trying to be everywhere at once. With the flight gone, I returned to my quarters, not exactly luxurious for a leggy fellow, but smelling pleasantly of the two oranges I'd left on my pillow. I picked them up, stashed one behind a book and began to peel the other, sitting on my bunk. Beside the oranges I had left a blue envelope. I picked it up, sniffed the perfume and smiled. Like a drunkard who lets his whiskey sit on the bar, savoring it, I had put aside the letter from my wife, hoping to consume it in little sips. I swung my feet up and turned on the reading light.

Dear Mike,

I don't know why the Lord made me a woman and then let me marry a bastard who's never here when I need him, which is damn near every night. Don't be surprised, when you come home, to find I've gone off with the grocery boy or the new minister at church who is over seventy but still gives the choir girls the eye.

As for your two darling daughters, they are driving me nuts. Emily, your precious perfect Emily, sweet fourteen and never been kissed. (Ha!) She came home Sunday a.m. at *two* o'clock. Zero-two-hundred to you, Lieutenant. She had been riding on a motorcycle with a boy sailor, who smelled of gin. How about *that*, dear Daddy? And *defiant* when I told her to go to her room. What she needs is a spanking, but she's too big and you're too chicken even if you were here. I just wish you *had* been here—at least the sailor would have saluted instead of grinning like an ape and sputtering down the driveway on that disgusting machine.

As for Lucy, all *she* does is sit behind closed doors in her room, play phonograph records, and talk on the phone. Her grades are abominable and she couldn't care less. In talking to me her vocabulary has shrunk to two words; "Oh, Mother." This covers every possible situation. I have no doubt if I rushed into the room in the middle of the night yelling, "The house is on fire!" her response would be "Oh, Mother," which all goes to prove that the *status* here in San Diego is still *quo* and you're a lucky sea dog to be out there among the friendly Japanese.

I miss you, Mike. Come on home.

    Love,
    Maggie

I read the letter again, sniffing it like an old hound. She was right. I should be home doing my duty as a father and husband, instead of following Fritz around the Pacific. Maybe soon. God! What I wouldn't give to have her here in my arms!

Ship's bell struck the half hour and brought back a sudden memory. Maggie and I becalmed in a pea-soup fog in our sloop off the coast of Maine. Somewhere, a bell buoy was ringing mournfully and I had been grumbling for an hour. She had come up out of the cabin and said, "Quit grousing and let's make a little hay before the sun shines."

I said, stupidly, "We're in a sea lane, Maggie. Somebody's got to be topside."

She chuckled, "You be topside, lover. I'll be bottomside."

"But suppose a liner came along?"

She had laughed. "What a way to go!"

When we had made love, she lay quietly for a while as we listened to the buoy, the cries of lost sea gulls, the slap of lines against the mast, and the creak of the gently swaying boom. "You are the greatest," she said. "Stay home and we'll do that every night."

I wished to hell I had.

I could still picture the scene with Maggie when I told her I was volunteering for the Navy. We were living in New York's Gramercy Park and I was writing advertisements for an advertising agency. Our income was fairly substantial and our life-style was full of promise as well as day to day pleasures. We had started humbly, in a one-room apartment over a restaurant on 8th Street when I was earning only $15 a week as an office boy. So the agency salary seemed unusually large; conversely the Navy pay seemed very small and inadequate.

She listened without comment as I said that Fritz Rawlings, an old friend and professional naval officer, thought he could get me in the Jacksonville Navy pilots' school.

"Have you noticed," she said, "that there are four people in this apartment? Me, your charming wife, and two little girls whom we have taught to expect three meals a day."

I smiled. "I've noticed these people. In fact, I love them."

She nodded, as if she knew that. "Would it be rude to remind you, sir, that you have undertaken to support these females?"

"Not at all," I said, still smiling. "That has been—still is—my intention. Thousands of naval officers support their families."

"True," she replied. "I doubt if the list includes dead aviators."

Suddenly, our dialogue seemed artificial and repugnant. She rushed across the room and put her arms around me. "Don't do it, Mike. *Please*, don't do it."

For the first time—literally—in years, she broke into sobs. I was flabbergasted. She'd always been so resolute, so strong. "I'll handle this" was such a familiar statement I was lulled into a feeling that she could handle anything. Now, held tight by her arms, and torn by her sobs, I was reduced to pressing her glossy black hair against my chest and fumbling for words. Every time I started to say something like, "It's my duty," it seemed ridiculous.

When she had calmed down, I busied myself getting a box of Kleenex from the bathroom. As I returned she grinned at me, that brave little grin that I recalled from her two child-bearings, and all of a sudden it was I who needed the Kleenex. What the hell was I trying to do anyway? Act like a hero? They weren't drafting fathers; what made me think I would be an addition to the war effort? I asked myself these questions aloud, as she sat silent in our book-lined library, her big brown eyes shining in the lamp light. Outside, the traffic hooted and beeped and the Third Avenue El rattled past. These were the reassuring sounds of my life, of New York, where the good salaries were, where this green-painted room was full of my favorite books and oil paintings we'd bought in Paris. This was where I belonged. Why the hell was I trying to escape?

You'd think, after such self-examination, that I would have gone on with my work at the agency and let the bachelors and professionals deal with the war. Looking back, as I'm doing now, I cannot recapture the mad zeal that possessed me at that time—a zeal that withstood Maggie's further tears and (later) anger and frustration.

When I cracked up the plane in Florida and lay in the hospital, she thought she had won. How could I tell her that my resolution had become even greater, in spite of this heaven-sent way out? I didn't try until I'd recovered and I was strong enough to tell her the truth. Her reaction was surprising; "Okay," she said, "if you want it that bad, we'll have to see that you get it."

She then proceeded to use all the influence she possessed—a congressional uncle on the Armed Services Committee. Even as I recall and write about these things today, I am filled with awe and gratitude. As I mulled them over in my bunk aboard *Sussex*, they made me groan.

I fell asleep for about forty minutes, awakened by McCord's summons to the main bridge. As usual, it was a model of orderliness—quartermaster in white at the wheel, officer of the day on the wing of the bridge, correctly dressed, glass in hand, inspecting everything from the main deck activities to nearby sea gulls. I felt somewhat out of uniform, having slept in my clothes. McCord, in freshly pressed shirt and trousers, ignored my wrinkles. The Captain handed me a dispatch. I glanced at the source and whistled. "El General!"

"The man himself."

I adjusted my glasses and got the typing into sharp focus. "Henceforth, the commanding officer of the carrier will refrain from arbitrary cancellation of prearranged flights in support of land operations vital to success of Philippine liberation. I require full air support beginning at zero-six-hundred tomorrow morning." He gave the beach and its exact location. "Acknowledge."

"No 'please?'" I handed it back, shaking my head.

The Captain said, "You know damn well our boys won't be ready for another attack tomorrow morning. If they find the battleship today, they'll be needing all kinds of R and R, God knows. If they don't find him, they'll still be dead beat. Maybe even coming back after dark." He looked up at the late afternoon sky.

I shared his concern, maybe it was the scene with Stone or maybe it was the earlier discussion with the Admiral about darkness. I was getting worried. "Want me to take the dispatch down to flag?" The Captain shook his head. "Not yet. Let's see how the flight's doing first. No use getting him all riled up if we don't have to."

"Going to answer?"

"You bet."

Evidently he'd already summoned his yeoman, who arrived breathless, pen in hand. "To the Supreme Allied Commander," the Captain began, with a mischievous twinkle in his eye. "Yours received by *Sussex.* Respectfully request replacing our air support with flight from many available carriers in this area. Our flight of 85 aircraft currently launched in search of reported enemy battleship cruisers and destroyers. Outcome as yet unknown. Availability at zero-six-hundred tomorrow extremely doubtful."

I couldn't resist a presumptuous: "Well done, sir."

McCord chuckled, "Probably get me fired. It's a cinch I'll never make Admiral if MacArthur had a vote." He looked at his wristwatch and walked out on the wing of the bridge, aiming his binoculars in a southeasterly direction. I could almost hear him muttering, "Come on, boys. It's getting late."

# Four

*Massive gray presence*
*moves into harm's way.*
*Beware the lone spear-thrower.*

The battleship *Amato* steamed west at flank speed. She had departed Truk in the Mariannas on urgent instructions and had turned her raked bow towards the Philippines. Word had come through naval intelligence that MacArthur had moved up his date for the invasion and *Amato's* guns were part of the frantic effort to stop him.

High in her pagoda-shaped bridge structure, Captain Osaka studied his charts. A small quiet man, the Captain wielded the 88,000-ton vessel as a samurai sword against his country's enemies. First in his class at the Naval Academy, and a descendant of ancient warriors, Osaka was proud to be the commander of one of Japan's great ships. He surveyed his accompanying squadron with affection. On station dead ahead, two sleek, fast destroyers; flanking him on either side, two heavy cruisers; astern, three more destroyers and a large supply vessel. A formidable task force with a glaring weakness. Air cover. Since Midway the Japanese Navy had not had an operating carrier at sea. Her fleet units went virtually naked when they cruised beyond the range of Japanese land-based aircraft.

As Osaka continued to study the charts, rain struck the thick glass of the main bridge, sluicing along sideways as the forward speed of the ship pressed against the glass. The Captain rolled up his charts and stood looking down at the water deluging the outer wing of the bridge. He thought of his hillside garden in summer, when the storms blew in from the ocean, making the half-buried rocks shine as if lacquered. He thought of peonies nodding to one another in the breeze and wondered if his wife was now plucking ants from the pink blooms.

Seated at his console, the Captain took out a folded letter and held it under the light. Around him he could hear the hum of the overhead wireless, the whine of wind across wires, the slow catarrhal breathing of the quartermaster, the hushed voice of the young duty officer on the phone. He read:

Dear Father:

I write you to say that I've been briefly in Tokyo and Mother seemed well.

We are very proud that you are commander of *Amato*. Little brother is talking of joining army air. How can the son of a naval family consider such a thing: He is only sixteen.

I am becoming a naval flier and greatly enjoy the sensation of being up in the air like a bird. How I would love to be with you and hear what happened at Midway. And I would also like to be again with you and Mother and Niki and Miro in our summer cottage and watch the moon rise and listen to mother making haiku and go sailing with Niki and Miro. Perhaps some day. If you see Miro tell him to behave.

Your loving son,
Kenishi (Ens.)

"Torpedoes off starboard bow!"

The lookout's cry galvanized *Amato*. The Captain dropped the letter and ran to the starboard wing of the bridge, as the watch officer called for General Quarters. The Captain's glasses picked up twin white wakes cutting through the dark water. "Hard right," he called at the door of the wheelhouse.

"Aye, sir," rumbled the heavy voice of the quartermaster as he swung the wheel. "Coming right."

Thousands of men ran to battle stations, strapping on life jackets, clamping down helmets, arming guns, carrying ammunition, clearing fire hoses. *Amato* heeled over as she swung toward the incoming shots. The Captain watched the wakes, noticed they were close together; a good sign. Trying to calculate the point where *Amato's* course and theirs would intersect, he realized that the ship was on a collision course. As he watched, his flanking squadron turned with him, like dancers in a slow measure. The wakes were closing fast.

Suddenly the lead destroyer, almost on her beam ends, put herself in the path of the torpedoes. "No!" the Captain growled as the gray hull of the destroyer blanked out the sight of the wakes. Then, with heart pounding, he said, "Miro!" Double explosions and a column of red and orange rose from the destroyer's midsection, as a thunderous blast washed against the bridge. The explosion broke the small ship's back and thrust her against *Amato*. From the outer edge of the formation came three more thumps, as picket destroyers depth-bombed the submarine.

Captain Osaka, swallowing hard, took the public address system. "*Agato* has been hit. Stand by for rescue operations."

Another heavy explosion from deep inside the damaged ship. Thick smoke now boiled out of her. Sailors began jumping into the sea. The Captain called, "All engines stop."

"Aye, sir."

"All engines stop."

The Captain snapped on his short wave radio. "*Amato* calling *Agato*." No need for the codes of silence here. "Commander Bonduri, this is Captain Osaka. Come in, please."

A voice crackling through static came on. "This is Lieutenant Shumari, sir. The Captain is dead. Sorry, sir." Osaka took a deep breath. "Are you seaworthy, Lieutenant? We are standing by."

"Sir, our engine room is flooded. Damage control says we are taking water badly there. *Not* seaworthy, sir. Sorry."

"Get your people off at once, Lieutenant."

"Aye, sir."

Captain thought for a moment. "That means you, too, Lieutenant. You weren't the Captain. Do you read me, Lieutenant?"

"Aye, sir."

What the Captain was yearning to say was: "Ensign Miro Osaka—is he all right?"

*Amato* was forced to back away as the fire increased. Men continued to leap off the destroyer and the battleship's strong boats hauled them aboard. Meanwhile, the depth bombing continued, with the squadron patrolling in circles. Osaka was torn between the urgency of his instructions and the delay of the rescue. At last, his executive officer reported all clear. Forty-four dead, 10 missing, 21 wounded. The rest okay.

Among the rescued who climbed the cargo net to board *Amato* was a young man with a broad grin, Ensign Osaka. The Captain greeted him formally in the presence of other officers.

Osaka returned to the bridge. "Please have the cruiser sink her." The squadron reformed, leaving the cruiser behind. Within five minutes Osaka could hear heavy guns firing. Looking back he saw the destroyer disappearing. Time now for what lies ahead.

In his sea cabin the Captain embraced his son, who—with his father's arms around him — broke down and wept. The older man allowed him to do so, then handed him a folded handkerchief, meaning "enough."

"For the moment," the Captain said, "You will be assigned to *Amato*. I'll have the orders cut. Then you will be sent home for rest and recuperation, your ship having been sunk."

The small slender Ensign dried his eyes and stood at attention in the presence of a senior officer, who said, "Relax, Miro. Your Mother will be glad to see you."       "Thank you, sir."

Captain Osaka smiled. "How about, 'Thank you, Father'?"

"Thank you, Father."

"Good. Now go find some dry clothes."

Night, and the great warship plunged massively into rising seas. In the Captain's cabin, dinner for two, perfectly served by white-coated attendants. Dining with the Captain, Ensign Miro Osaka, late of the destroyer *Agato*, dressed in a new blue uniform, was very proud. Father and son at a small table, flowers in the center, two ancient scrolls on the bulkhead. The water level in the flower vase moved as the ship wrestled with the wind and waves. The father smiled, as he watched the son eat a serving of baked fish.

"Didn't they feed you on *Agato*?"

"Oh, yes, sir."

"A swim in the ocean makes you hungry?"

"Yes, sir."

A brief pause as they both thought of the torpedo and the sinking.

"Lose many friends?" the father asked.

"Yes, sir. Especially Commander Bonduri."

"Good man. I'll write his wife. Such a shame!"

"Of course, sir."

"You flew out to Truk to join *Agato*. Were you home before that?"

"Yes, sir. Mother is fine. Very busy with the hospital work, and the flowers. Cheerful."

They paused while the mighty ship plunged ahead in the surging darkness.

"How do you like the Navy, Miro?"

"I love the Navy, sir. When the war is over, perhaps I can return to college, then make it my career."

"When the war is over, my boy, I doubt if there will be a Japanese Navy. If you return to college, become a doctor, a lawyer, or engineer."

The remark shocked Ensign Osaka. His father, the family hero, had never hinted at such things before. Miro was speechless for a moment. Then, "Are we losing, sir?"

"We are losing, my boy. But they will pay heavily before we give up."

The boy struck the table with his fist. "How can this be?"

"More ships, Miro. More planes, more bombs, more Marines, Army, Air Force, everything."

The Ensign fell silent, feeling a shiver of fear, which was unusual in the presence of his father.

# Five

One thing was fortunate. As an old college track runner I had strong legs, which served me well as I ran up and down the ladders between main bridge and flag bridge, otherwise known as the rock, the Captain, and the hard place, the Admiral—a phrase created by Fritz while kidding me about the assignment in which I was caught.

On the flag bridge I watched the old man pace the bridge with his face always turned to the empty southeast horizon. The Chief of Staff bent over his chart, pipe in hand. I merely stood by in case the old man wanted information about the flight.

Funny the way the twilight appeared. Our watch told us it was time, but daylight was still with us. Then, almost as if someone had turned a rheostat, it started fading fast. Maybe five minutes passed before the Admiral noticed the change. When he realized what was happening, he came to me and said, rather accusingly, "Goddamnit, Mike, where are they? It's getting late."

One thing was obvious: They hadn't found the Japs, or they'd have alerted us long ago.

I decided to try some facts on the Admiral that I assumed he knew—but maybe not. "We don't really want them now—do we, sir? Not for at least thirty minutes."

He cocked his head on the side and said, "What the hell are you talking about?"

"Just reminding the Admiral that twilight isn't supposed to be a good time for carrier landings. Don't they call it a 'pinkie'? Seems it's hard to keep a perspective. The group has lost three fliers landing in pinkies."

"You telling me I'd do better in pitch black than right now?"

"That's what they say, sir."

"Bullshit. And how long does this stupid time last—this pinkie?"

"Depends, Admiral. Here I'd say it'll be truly dark in 30 minutes.
"That right, Stowell?"

The Chief of Staff removed his pipe. "Right." He smoked *Barking Dog* tobacco in his pipe. Flag plot was full of it and I loved the smell.

The Admiral growled and resumed his patrol of the bridge. Except for a following destroyer and our two anti-submarine cans up ahead, we seemed to be alone on the great green ocean. Yet just over the horizon, spreading for countless miles, I knew a huge armada gathered. In it were thousands of Marines and Army fighting men, armed and ready to retake the Philippines, probably sweating in hot troopships interspersed with cruisers, destroyers, and various landing craft. Dozens of carriers steamed westward with them—all under our Admiral's command. We were on our way to victory, but we hadn't fully reckoned with the Japanese.

Although I hadn't convinced the Admiral that pinkie was the wrong time to recapture our planes, I was glad when the last evidence of the sun was gone from the west. Captain Stowell stuck his head in from the wing of the bridge. "I heard them, Admiral."

"Good."

Almost as he spoke, the great ship turned into the wind and the bow started to rise and fall. The LSO paddles became a Ping-Pong game waiting to be played in the dark near the stern. The flight deck emerged from black with its parallel blue lines and the voice of the air boss boomed out. "Stand by to receive aircraft. Clear the flight deck. Look alive. Planes coming aboard. Stand by LSOs."

I climbed back up to the main bridge, figuring with the group returning, that's where I'd be the busiest. Looking back on what happened, it's remarkable that the first three planes came aboard without a hitch. One, two, three down, unhooked and moved forward out of the way—as if it were a day of exercise with no pressure.

Then the trouble started. Suddenly, above us in the dark, a desperate voice on the radio. "Help! Outta gas. Fuel negative. Can't make it. Oh, shit! Air Group One Thirteen. This is TBF Eleven. Ditching."

I swallowed hard. I stood on the bridge with the Captain who quietly asked, "Who is TBF Eleven?"

"Adams, sir. Tommy Adams."

The air boss called, "We copy. Keep your nose up. Put her down near the destroyer. Repeat. Make your water landing near the can. Stay cool, Tommy."

"Roger Willco. Hope they're listening."

A new voice came over the air from the destroyer: "We copy.

Swimmers are in the water. Luck, TBF Eleven."

For a long minute we heard nothing. Then the destroyer voice again, "TBF's down. Swimmers deployed... aircraft starting to sink... canopy still in place... TBF going under. Swimmers with it... swimmers up..." The voice stopped then continued with a change of tone, "No pilot. Sorry."

The air boss came back: "Resume recovering aircraft."

Six planes came in successfully, sputtering and yawing, their exhaust burning white and blue in the dark. A second desperate voice reached us, as the Captain said, "No," and clenched his fist. "Where's the fucking ship?  Fuel negative, you hear. No goddamn gas. Help me, somebody."

Then still another voice. "Where are you *Sussex*? For God's sake, where? Fuel... "

Sudden footsteps sounded on the ladder from flag plot. Glasses in hand and eyes blazing, the Admiral came running up, out of breath. "Turn on the lights, McCord."

The Captain shook his head, "Can't do that, Admiral."

"Why the hell not?"

"Enemy subs, sir. We're a big target."

"Fuck the subs, Captain. Do it!"

"You're endangering 3,000 men, Admiral."

The Admiral took a deep breath. "I want you to turn on your lights, Captain."

"Wait a minute, sir."

"No time to argue."

"I won't accept responsibility for... "

"Fuck responsibility." The Admiral continued in a slow, deliberate voice, "I'm ordering you Captain McCord, turn-on-the-fucking-lights."

McCord, cool, calm and ultimately realistic, quietly said, "Aye, sir."

In a normal voice he called the air boss who put the order on the air. "Now here this. Light the ship. Repeat. Turn on all deck lights. Destroyers turn on search lights."

Hardly had his voice ceased than two unseen fliers overlapping called, "Out of gas. Going in. Can't make it. Fuel negative. Help."

The Admiral strode to the end of the bridge, peering down. One fighter splashed near the destroyer. Swimmers reached his aircraft in seconds and the cockpit cover came off. As the F6F started to sink the pilot emerged and shrugged out of his parachute. The two black suited swimmers took him under both arms and made their way back to the destroyer.

A dive bomber, high and fast, came in for a landing and got a wave-off. On his second try he came down hard and bounced. Still carrying his speed, he missed the hook and swerved to the right, skipping off the deck and into the gun tubs. Suddenly he caught fire. The pilot popped his canopy, scrambled out. In seconds a major fire was raging with his fifties about to go off.

The air boss called out, "All aircraft, deck emergency. Knock off landing and continue circling. Fire on deck. Fire on deck."

A small voice came out of the dark. "Hellcat Forty-four. Air Group One Thirteen. Fuel negative. Request permission for priority landing."

The air boss response was quiet. "Hellcat Forty-four, permission denied. Deck closed. Repeat. Permission refused."

The voice, now recognizable. "Please, sir. I got no gas. *Por favor.*" It was Martinez. God be with us.

A new voice—Fritz Rawlings'. "Martinez! Do you read me? This is Rawlings."

"Yes, sir, I read. For God's sake, Commander—Help me. Please."

Fritz cut across him. "Listen, Marty. *Listen to me.* Get your canopy open."

"But, sir."

"Put her down *now,* Marty. *Now.* She will last for twenty seconds without gas and no bombs. Get as close to the can as possible. Crawl out fast just like we practiced. Get rid of the chute. Take your flashlight. The swimmers will pick you up. *Do it, Martinez!*"

In a subdued voice the answer, "Okay, sir. *Madre de Dios.*"

I crossed to the other wing of the bridge to watch. My heart was going fast. Under the lights the two swimmers in wet suits looked like seals. Marty's big blue fighter, wobbling and yawing, hit the water, bounced headfirst into a wave and turned over. The two swimmers reached the aircraft in seconds and both men dived. In another few seconds the canopy came off. Then after a long interlude, both swimmers emerged for air and dived back. The aircraft began to sink, slipping down sideways. In a sudden upward burst of released air both swimmers surfaced carrying Martinez, who seemed unconscious. They ferried his limp body to the destroyer. A sling was lowered from the deck and Martinez was carefully lifted aboard. I let out a huge sigh. So much for flying with a rosary.

I expected Fritz any minute, but he evidently wanted to get as many people aboard as he could while his fuel lasted. In ten minutes the deck fire was out.

A thin voice crackled in our ears, interrupted by the spitting sound of broken transmission. "Hello *Sussex*... "

"I can see your lights... but I can't get... there... negative... fuel... bone dry. TBF Sixteen going in... don't know where I am. Help!"

Four more fighters landed safely. Then Stone's harsh voice, "This is Torpecker Nine. I'm burning air but I made it. Coming aboard."

Air boss boomed, "Permission to land, Torpecker Nine. The deck is clear."

Stone brought down the sputtering engine smoothly, rolled to a stop, released the trip wires and cleared the area. In ten minutes, helmet in hand, he came charging up the ladder and burst into the main bridge. Not bothering to salute, he marched up to the surprised Captain and said, "Sir, I demand that Commander Rawlings be replaced as CAG of this outfit."

"Who are you?" the Captain asked, quietly.

"I'm Jesse Stone, sir, squadron leader of the torpedo bombers."

"You're out of line, Stone."

"Fuck that, sir. Rawlings has killed Christ knows how many guys of One Thirteen because he wouldn't turn back soon enough. Our people have run outa gas and ditched all over the goddamn ocean and it's his fucking fault."

The Captain said, "That's enough, Lieutenant. There's a place for such charges. Not here."

"He's an irresponsible idiot, sir. I'm telling the Captain."

McCord raised his voice. "You're dismissed, Stone."

"Sir, you gotta do something. This here man... "

"Get out," the Captain growled. "Now!"

I watched Stone turn pale under his tan. He spun around and stepped through the door. We could hear his boots on the ladder, each one a hammer blow.

The Captain said, "When Rawlings lands, ask him to come up here will you, Mason?"

"Aye, sir."

"What's the Navy come to?" he asked.

A purely rhetorical question, I figured.

Two more aircraft ditched; the destroyer swimmers saved one, lost one. When the aircraft sank in a mass of bubbles that shone in the light, I could imagine the young pilot trapped inside, choked with sea water and then drifting down in the darkness, down for two or three *miles*. God! It made me want to yell: "Stop this! Call it off!"

The Captain paced his bridge, searching the illuminated areas for the tell-tale signs of an incoming torpedo, checking his wrist watch. "How many does that make, Mike?"

"More than about half of 'em, sir. Fifty-four."

In the next twenty minutes two more splashed, were picked up and six came aboard successfully.

The Captain apparently made a decision. "Follow me," he said. To the officer of the deck, "Take the con."

"Aye, sir," the officer of the deck said.

We found the Admiral wiping sweat from his face. "Well?" The old man peered over the handkerchief.

"I respectfully request that the Admiral allow us to darken ship. We have been lighted now for over thirty minutes and I cannot allow *Sussex* to remain in danger of submarine attack any longer."

The Admiral cleared his throat, and tucked away the handkerchief in his pants pocket. "Appreciate your concern, Captain. I'm worried too. But look at what's happening. They're still ditching the goddamn planes. That fellow just said he was 'burning air'. They're *all* burning air, tonight. Went too far before they started back."

"We know that, sir. My fault. He expected us to make more distance closing with him. But the heavy seas slowed us down."

"I said it before, McCord. We have to take our risks. Name of the game."

In a reasonable tone the Captain said, "The lights, Admiral?"

The old man rubbed his chin. "How many still out there?"

"About ten aircraft, Admiral," I said.

"Suppose you were one of them?"

I wasn't sure whether he meant me or the Captain. I waited and McCord said, "I've been out there, sir. All of us have. It comes with the job—as you say."

"Give 'em five more minutes, McCord. Just five more minutes."

"Very well, sir. Thank you."

We returned to the main bridge, acutely aware now of time passing. Six aircraft came aboard including Terry Vernon with a sputtering engine. The seventh ditched and its pilot was picked up. Last of the six was Fritz's big blue fighter gliding down for a landing. The Captain gave me a signal with a head movement, and I took off to find Fritz and caught him coming out of the head, zipping up his pants. We shook hands. "Captain wants you."

He nodded. "Figures."

I said, "Our buddy Stone came up and blew his top."

"That little bastard."

"He accused you of irresponsibility and demanded your replacement."

Looking tired, with deep circles under his eyes Rawlings let his shoulders slump—an unfamiliar attitude. "Maybe he's right. And the Captain?"

"Said Stone was out of line. Told him to get lost."

"Did he?"

"Mac wants to see you."

"Why not? I really fucked up."

I figured neither Fritz nor the Captain wanted a witness for this meeting so I returned to flag country. No more aircraft had come aboard. As time ran out the air boss' voice boomed. "Darken ship. Destroyers. Copy. Darken ship. Darken ship." In an instant black night recaptured the great ship, flanked by protective destroyers. Now we sailed in darkness, broken only by twin blue lines on the deck and the no-longer-useful paddles of the LSOs. Standing on the bridge in the humid night I listened for the late-comers, praying for the sputter of an engine, the sudden radio voice of a lost bird calling for help. Nothing–only the whistle of wind, and the distant crunch of bow waves.

"How many did we lose?" the Admiral asked.

I consulted my notes. "Four torpeckers and four pilots, three dive bombers and one pilot, and four fighters and two pilots."

"Total seven pilots, eleven planes," the Chief of Staff said.

"Yes, sir."

The Admiral shook his head and crushed out a cigarette. "All for nothing. Seven men, eleven planes and still not a shot at the goddamn battleship. Where did he go?"

"Hard to say, sir," Stowell said. "They could have had a search plane that found us without being spotted. They could have had a sub that gave them a warning. In either case, they could have turned north and we'd have missed them."

The Admiral studied the chart. "Something scared them off. That's for sure. What have they got left?"

"Well, sir," Stowell answered, "as you know, at Midway they lost *Akagi, Kaga, Hiryu,* and *Soryu.*"

"In other words they have no real carrier task force. Couple of CVs. That it?"

"More or less, sir. We hear it's four light ones."

"So if we sink their battleships and cruiser, we have 'em."

I wasn't so sure.

Stowell handed the Admiral a new report which he studied in apparent distaste. "Chickenshit stuff what the other ships did today."

The Chief of Staff smiled.

"Waste of man power and gasoline," the Admiral growled. "My wife could do more damage with a croquet mallet."

The Chief of Staff was not impressed. He put away his pipe and waited for orders.

"Take a message to all units. Enemy ships sighted. Give 'em date and last position. Bearing, speed, so on. One BB, two cruisers, two destroyers. Prepare to start two-stage search zero-two-thirty. Arm anti-shipping. Be ready to launch the search on my instructions."
Captain Stowell wrote it down carefully, said goodnight, and left for the radio shack. The old man took off his glasses and went slowly down the ladder. I hoped he'd get some rest. Tomorrow would be another killer.

Soon almost everybody slept—all men who had flown and recovered planes, pumped gas, hoisted bombs, replaced spark plugs, cooked soup, scrubbed pans, watched radar, radioed messages, oiled engines, dumped garbage, heard confessions, cut hair, scooped ice cream and run tractors. Worried as I was about Fritz, I finally hit the sack and joined them. As I dozed off I could feel the slow lifting and falling and could see in my mind the great ship moving without lights, under the big stars of the tropics, a huge presence in the darkness with her great engines throbbing deep inside, and wireless crackling high like crickets up above the island, bow waves crumpling, and a phosphorescent wake unraveling astern like a dusty white road.

# Six

*Old hawk circling*
*Wonders where the field mice went.*
*Drafted by High Command?*

The Mitsubishi passenger aircraft bumped through warm updrafts over the Philippine Sea like an oxcart on a rocky road. Admiral Ishino, a veteran aviator, ignored the roughness as he spoke to his aide just loud enough to be heard above the propellers, but inaudible to the pilot.

"I knew they would see it finally. Let's pray it's not too late."

The aide said, "The crowd in Tokyo is usually too late."

Admiral Ishino crushed his cigarette and the aide held a lighter for the next one. "What about the young fliers, sir? Do you think they will volunteer?"

The Admiral drew deep, coughed, spoke through the smoke, "I cannot order them to die."

The aide stared down at the sea, which was dotted with small islands. "Actually, we're all committed to do that."

The Admiral nodded. "Theoretically, yes. But volunteering to fly an aircraft into an enemy ship—that's not theoretical."

"Is the situation really that bad, sir? Asking kids to kill themselves?"

"Bad enough. We lost most of our carriers at Midway, but—as I told those people—be realistic. We don't *need* the carriers. The enemy has come to us. He can be reached and destroyed from *land* bases."

The Admiral pointed to the islands below. "Land bases everywhere, but damned few trained pilots. I want the few we have left to inflict the most damage."

The plane circled to land. Again the Admiral crushed his cigarette, fixed his seat belt, peered at the landing field which was surrounded by thick shrubbery on one side and woods on the other. The landing strip was pock-marked with fresh earth. "I see we've had some visitors," the Admiral said.

As the plane rolled to a squeaking stop, a stream of young men in khaki poured out of a nearby wooden building and ran forward. As they reached the edge of the runway, they halted and lined up in two columns. In front of them an older pilot in the tan summer uniform of a Lieutenant Commander, marching with a cane, brought them to attention. He then turned, with a slight stumble, and saluted the Admiral, who returned the salute. The two officers bowed; as did the Admiral's aide, a Navy captain.

The Lieutenant Commander spoke. "Welcome, sir, to the 200th Special Attack Unit."

The two columns of men bowed. Again the old pilot bowed and smiled. "Thank you, gentlemen. I am happy to be with you."

The wail of the air raid siren abruptly ended further ceremony. "Take cover," called the Lieutenant Commander. The young men ran for the woods. The Admiral followed them at a more dignified pace, guided by the Lieutenant Commander. The aide modified his speed to that of the Admiral. They had barely reached the trees when a stream of huge F6Fs began diving down and peppering the field with .50 caliber machine gun rounds. Several Hellcats dropped 250-pound bombs on rivetted Zeroes that were actually wooden dummies. Spurts of earth jumped up everywhere. Bullets ricocheted off cement surfaces. A small petrol tank went up with an ear-splitting crack. Defensive ground fire rattled away when the gunners reached their weapons. It was all over in ten minutes. As if the rain were a curtain closing the attack, a squall blew in off the sea, sluicing the runway, turning the fresh bomb hits into muddy pits.

The attack over, the unit reassembled and the Admiral, in his damp and wrinkled uniform, stood before the young men. For a brief moment he merely looked at them, moving his eyes from face to face. The only sound in the room was rain tapping on the corrugated metal roof and gurgling in the gutter. The air smelled of cordite from the bombs and sweat from the bodies. "I am flattered that the enemy also came to welcome me."

Laughter. Nobody expected an Admiral to be amusing. He let his face grow serious, as the laughter died.

"Gentlemen. I don't enjoy making speeches. Like you, I am a flier. But there comes a time when talk is necessary."

He paused, coughed; out of the corner of his eye he could see men running with buckets of earth and crushed stone to repair the runways. "The enemy is about to land at Leyte gulf. We have no real carriers to stop him. If he takes the Philippines, he is within easy striking distance of the home islands. I said we have no real carriers, but," he paused, *"we don't need carriers.* We can destroy the enemy ships with land-based aircraft. Not in conventional attacks; their pilots are too skilled for that. Conventional air defense—won't work with untrained pilots. A man who has flown a few training hours can't fight a battle-tested veteran. Indeed, he can barely return to his own airfield."

Again a ripple of laughter mingled with the rain and the sudden whine of metal being cut in the repair shops. The Admiral continued. "On the other hand, a single Zero carrying a 250-pound bomb can blow a destroyer in half, knock out a cruiser's bridge, dive down an elevator and put a carrier out of action. What I'm saying, gentlemen, is this: We can stop the enemy if—our pilots will dive their aircraft into the ships."

Deep silence followed his words. He smothered a cough. The young fliers sat without speaking, each occupied with his own thoughts. The Admiral cleared his throat. "I have just come from Tokyo where this action was approved by the general staff and brought to the attention of the Emperor. I am very proud that you—the 200th—have been offered the privilege of considering whether you wish to be part of such a program. Indeed, to lead it. When we join the armed forces, I suppose each of us dreams of distinction, a chance for courage, perhaps even a moment to die for the Emperor." His voice trembled with emotion as he looked into the eyes of the rapt youngsters. "This is such a moment. This is your opportunity—literally and gloriously—to die for your Emperor—and strike a unique and terrifying blow against the enemy."

A young man in the front row leaped to his feet. "I am ready, sir."

The Admiral smiled. "I appreciate your enthusiasm, son. But let's take our time. Talk to your friends. Think long and hard. Make up your mind in private."

The young officer sat down, somewhat abashed.

The Admiral said, "Tomorrow, I shall talk further with those of you who have volunteered."

He bowed and walked out of the room as the pilots rose to their feet.

A special room had been set aside for the Admiral in a Quonset hut. His aides bunked with the Lieutenant Commander. Partially undressed, the Admiral lay on his cot staring at the curved metal ceiling and listening to the rain. A night bird kept squawking as though someone were torturing it. What was it? Parrot? Ishino had little doubt that the unit would volunteer. This should have elated him. Instead, it filled him with sadness. So many eager young men about to die. His idea. Applauded by the high command—all of whom slept in clean dry comfortable beds and had no intention of diving to their death.

Would the sacrifices do any good the Admiral wondered? Sink a few carriers. Kill a few hundred men. In the long run could the kamikazes do anything but delay the inevitable? Admiral Ishino turned over on his lumpy cot, wincing at the stab of pain in his lower back. There was no comfortable position; why *should* there be? Tomorrow they would volunteer and—one by one, go to their deaths—while he, the author of it all, would be back in his comfortable home on the outskirts of Tokyo with all the useless members of his high command. Everybody in perfect comfort—with servants and soft pillows and the occasional smiles of Hirohito to spur them on.

The rain increased and the Admiral could now hear the regular tapping of a leak somewhere in the room. He didn't care as long as it wasn't directly over the bed. He thought of his wife, now dead these dozen years. Could he have ever been the strong young officer who raced down the beach with her and carried her easily into the bridal chamber as if she were a kitten. Would he ever see her again? The young fliers—some of them—believed their sacrifice would take them to the Emperor's garden. Did he believe that? He doubted it; doubted that there was anything but oblivion. The night was long.

# Seven

*Old pelican, having caught*
*ten thousand fish,*
*smells of authority.*

Admiral Ishino smiled, in spite of a backache, in spite of another Hellcat attack, in spite of constant rain. Before him, also smiling, stood the Lieutenant Commander with his cane. He had just reported to the Admiral that every man in the 200th Special Attack Unit had volunteered.

The Admiral slapped his palms together. "I knew it. I knew they'd do it."

The Lieutenant Commander bowed. "If the Admiral pleases, I should like to be their leader."

The Admiral shook his head. "No, no, my dear fellow. We need you here. We need a training officer who has been to war. Not some milksop who read a few books on how to fly. Stay here and teach them to be warriors."

The older pilot persisted. "I owe the enemy a blow, sir."

The Admiral brushed the comment aside. "So do I. So does everybody, son. You'll hit them harder with thirty accurate dives from these boys than anything you could do by yourself."

Frustrated, the Commander bowed.

"Please assemble the men," the Admiral said.

When they were seated and had quieted down, the Admiral began to speak so quietly that the men in the back row had to strain forward to catch every word.

"Gentlemen, I congratulate you. Every flier in the 200th has volunteered."

He paused to let them react, but they sat in silence, as if they were expecting it.

"I give you my word that your sacrifices will not be forgotten. The Emperor himself shall know." He coughed, "Let me give you some suggestions that may help you strike your enemy more effectively. There are two ways to approach an enemy warship. One from a great height—above their radar and combat air patrol, say 4,000 meters. When the target is sighted, *arm your bomb*. Don't do so beforehand because you may not find a ship, and you can't return to base and land with an armed bomb."

This seemed to amuse them. The old man went on. "Try to estimate wind direction. Watch which way the ship's smoke is blowing. Wind is important in your dive. Think about the kites of your childhood. Be careful the wind doesn't blow you past your target.

"Don't dive irrationally. You are intelligent men. Use your intelligence. For instance—attacking a carrier. The ideal attack is three-pronged. One strike into the forward elevator. One into aft elevator. One against the bridge. Coordinate your attacks."

Again he was taken with a fit of coughing. The room was filled with the tapping of rain and the occasional raucous cries of parrots in the trees. "The other approach," the Admiral said, "is low level. Come in fast, just above the water, too far down for radar or guns. They can only depress so much. Stay low until you're 200 meters from the ship. Then pull back and climb 1,000 meters. Pick your spot and dive." His tone hardened, "Fliers of 200th, I salute you. Kamikazes!"

Kenishi Osaka, aged nineteen, wished his father could have heard the Admiral. He'd have been very proud.

On his flight back to Tokyo the Admiral sat silently thinking of what he had created. He felt guilty to have conceived such a mission that would kill so many young men—with no personal risk to himself. He'd already had more than his share of risk, as a flier, as an aircraft group leader, a carrier executive officer. He was quietly fatalistic about the outcome of the war, now that the Americans were approaching in such force.

Almost as if on cue, two small American carriers appeared below in the mist. The pilot noticed them at the same time and quickly headed for a large cloudbank to the west. No anti-aircraft shells followed. Where was their combat air patrol? The Admiral smiled. So much for over confidence on the part of the enemy.

But it did remind him that his journeys to and from Tokyo were not entirely without peril. Somehow, considering his feelings of guilt at what he'd done, the thought brought a certain amount of comfort.

# Eight

Mid-morning. *Sussex* steamed into the wind, together with her sister ships and their destroyers and cruisers. The heat was oppressive, despite the breeze created by the ship's speed. The Admiral was standing on his bridge reading a message from MacArthur: "Urgent change of order #029. Task Force 485 will seal off the eastern exit of Mendova Strait using all forces to prevent emergence of enemy fleet units which could threaten landings."

The Admiral crumpled the dispatch in anger. "Typical bullshit. The enemy has already 'emerged!' Fucking General wants me to sit on my ass in the barnyard after the horse has run off. Let's have a look at that chart."

He followed me into flag plot, where Stowell bent over a large map of the approaches to the Philippines. Taking a red grease pencil, the Admiral made an X at the opening of the Mendova Strait, between the southern tip of Mangayan Island and the northern tip of Pindoro Point. "That's the barn door Doug wants me to slam. But I say it's too late. We were chasing the horse all day yesterday."

Captain Stowell said, "Suppose you're wrong, sir. General MacArthur may have fresh intelligence."

"Then let him fill us in, for chrissake. Send him a reminder of the two sub sightings yesterday. Say I'm leaving him three CVs to plug Mendova Strait, but *Sussex* will continue to hunt."

The old man lit a cigarette and spat out the smoke. "That group we're looking for could really fuck up a landing. Sonofabitch if I'm going to hang around Mendova waiting for ships that may never come out, with heavy Jap stuff already roaming around loose, ready to blow away our assault troops from ten miles off.

"Figure out coordinates for patrols off Mendova and assign stations to Gettysburg and the others. As for *Sussex*, let's make an assumption.

The Japs are smart. They know about the big landing in spite of the false move yesterday, and they're waiting for MacArthur to make his real move. When he does, they'll be there shelling the beach and the transports, and it's up to us to stop them." The Admiral looked into space, and his voice grew husky. "Where did they go? Where in the hell did those bastards go?"

Fritz came to me looking a little harried. "The Admiral wants me. Can you help me out? The can picked up five of our guys last night. Could you swing over to sick bay and see how they're doing? Particularly, Martinez. Let 'em know we care."

I was glad to talk to the kids. Wasn't too happy about the ride on the high line, but managed it with only one near-dousing when the two vessels leaned toward each other. The destroyer people helped me out of the crossing-gear, which looked like an old-fashioned deep sea diver outfit without the helmet, and off I went to sick bay. The difference in motion between the huge carrier and the 2,100-ton destroyer was quite noticeable. Luckily, my seasick days lay far behind me, sailing in the Chesapeake Bay.

I was greeted noisily by our five young fliers who had ditched, all of whom seemed none the worse for wear. I expected everybody to be in hospital outfits—white "skivveys" opening down the back. Instead all five were in Navy pants and shirts. I held up a hand and said, "I bring you greetings from Fritz Rawlings who's having a little chat with the Admiral. He said the cost of your aircraft will be taken out of your salary for the next fifty years."

They liked this and I felt happy to be among them. Somehow, they gave me the feeling—except for Martinez, whose skin was much darker—that they were all members of the same American family—short stiff hair, tanned faces, white teeth, typical American boys. I chatted with each of them, getting history, terrifying at the time, now, mostly the material for jokes. Martinez had suffered some sprains from the resuscitation efforts and had his ribs taped. Several other men wore bandages covering injuries from the desperate evacuation process. Basically they were not much worse off than a basketball team after a tough game. I checked with Martinez who was not quite as exuberant as his fellows. He stared at the deck. "I almost didn't make it last night. Couldn't pop the cover. Couldn't get out of the harness. Actually couldn't *think*. Just seemed to freeze."

"Lots of guys freeze. Scarey business."

"I really hit the panic button."

"I've done it myself. Know what you mean."

*"Bueno"* he said, grinning.

"Watching from the bridge it looked like you were going down with the plane."

"Damn near. I got tangled in the 'chute like an octopus. Thank God for those guys from the can. I thought I was going to die. I was breathing water. I mean it–like a fucking fish."

"I can believe it."

"The good Lord was watching."

"Absolutely." I wanted to ask about the rosary but decided not to.

"Tell me, Mr. Mason. I really fucked up, didn't I?"

"A lot of people did, Marty."

"But I was the worst. The air boss really slammed the door on me."

"It was a tricky time, Marty. He had a deck fire."

"I know. I must have sounded like an idiot."

"Forget it, Marty." A pause. The destroyer wasn't exactly a stable platform going through the waves. She rose and fell aggressively–much more than the huge carrier.

"Is Commander Rawlings burned up?"

"He's okay, Marty."

Marty shifted his position and winced.

"What's the matter?"

"My ribs. When they got me aboard I was full of water. They cracked a rib squeezing me dry."

"A cracked rib should get you Rest and Recuperation on Pearl."

Martinez shook his head. "No, sir. Please do me a favor. No R and R. Tell the Commander. No R and R. The rib hurts, but it won't keep me from flying. Promise me, sir? You'll tell him, no R and R?"

"You're crazy, Marty. You're turning down a chance to get back to Hawaii? Think it over. R and R in Pearl."

"Not for Martinez."

He looked at me fiercely. Neither of us spoke for the moment as the destroyer climbed another mountain and slid down the other side. "I'll tell him," I said. "But–he may not buy it."

I followed Fritz to his room. He flopped on the bunk and kicked off his flying boots. "How'd it go with Marty and the rest?" I sprawled in his only chair. "Not bad," I said. "He has a cracked rib. He damn near drowned and they squeezed him too hard getting the water out."

"Anybody else hurt?"

"Lots of scratches. Nothing serious. Surprise from Marty."

"Like what?"

"The rib could get him back to Pearl."

"Why not?"

"He doesn't want R and R. 'Please,' he says. 'No R and R!' He feels guilty for the way he lost it coming back."

"Don't blame him. But, hell, a lot of guys were out of order. The air boss has got to slap 'em around and get everybody aboard. I told Marty to forget it; easier said than done."

Fritz was in a reflective mood. "This job is a killer. Believe me, when this war is over I'm getting out. You think I want to be an admiral? Forget it. If I come through this war alive, I'm getting myself a sailboat and my boy and I—we're going down to Florida and take it easy."

"What about his mother?"

"She made her choice. She's getting herself a meal ticket. I'm taking the boy. We'll find us a house near the water, maybe on the Keys, and make up for lost time. I'll teach him to sail, fish, scuba dive—the works."

"What about college?"

He paused and stared into the distance. A pair of sailors went along the passageway, laughing. As he contemplated reality his voice changed. "I'm talking summers. Hell, I know he'll be going to college. Fancy prep school like his. All the kids 'll be Ivy Leaguers."

Fritz tossed me a letter.

Salisbury Academy

Dear Dad,

Well I made the team—just barely. Everybody outweighs me by maybe twenty pounds. You never saw such a bunch of horses. Good thing I can run. Been practicing my passing and am glad we had those days at the beach last summer when you and I did all that running and passing. You must have been pretty good at Annapolis. Too bad you didn't decide to play pro ball then I would have seen you a lot more.

Mom came to see me last weekend—with her new 'beau'. She looked okay but thinner and kind of nervous. He doesn't talk much. Not a bad guy but real old, maybe fifty. Gave me a twenty dollar bill. I felt funny accepting money from a stranger and handed it back. Mama gave me one of those looks—like she was going to kill me— and I took the money, which I sure can use, as am dead broke as usual.

Take care of yourself, Dad. I miss you.

Love,

Tom

P.S. Surprise! I just heard I'm starting quarterback tomorrow against St. Paul's. If you never hear from me again, it's because they killed me.

Fritz listened to me chuckling as I read his letter. When I finished, he said, "Great kid. I miss him... Loves to fish. One time in Back Bay..." He was off and running into the past. "It was early morning. A good time. Quiet. Cool. Still dark. Tom always liked it. Hated to wake up, but once he was awake, happy and eager to get started.

"Back Bay was covered with mist when we arrived. Tom loved the smell around the pier—the swamp's own special smell, dark water and cypress stumps, faintly fishy.

"Old man Whipple's geese were talking among themselves that time of day, and far out in the bay a motor. Now and then a fish plopped; otherwise nothing.

"Whipple was our guide. Without him you'd never find a fucking bass. Probably never get home. Back Bay's open water and narrow channels wind through cattails and marsh grass. Without a guide you could waste a whole day and never see anything but dragonflies and a hawk or two. Whipple was the best. He knew the place like the palm of his hand. Tom and I disturbed the geese and old man Whipple came out on the porch bare-footed, wearing a broken straw hat, a grey shirt and blue jeans, carrying two cokes and a sandwich in wax paper. Whipple nodded and led us through the wet grass to his boat. We had bamboo poles, casting rods, and a minnow bucket. He started the engine—loud as hell—and the old blunt-end flat bottom moved down the channel to the boat house, where we watched the old man scoop minnows out of the bait box and drop them in the bucket. Then down the main channel and across the bay as the sun came up, we took off. Tom sat in the bow facing forward. I sat amidships, feeling good about the boy, noticing how his shoulders were filling out.

"We had live bait, but started with plugs. Whipple cut the engine and pointed to the shore line. 'Yonder.' Tom's first cast went ashore, stuck on a reed. We paddled in to get it. Twice more he misjudged the distance. Then Whipple said, 'Might as well forget it here.' Tom was embarrassed.

"We drifted up to a duck blind. Whipple said, 'Big fellow under the box.' Tom picked up a minnow out of the bucket, hooked it through the tail. Swung the bamboo pole so that the minnow slipped under the box, where a duck hunter stood in the season. The cork bobbed along the edge of the box as the minnow moved. Suddenly the cork was yanked out of sight. 'There he is,' said Whipple. 'Let him chew it.'"

Fritz was caught up in his tale. He was there. "I remember the look on the boy's face. The cork came back in view on the far side of the blind, three inches below the surface, going away. Whipple turned the boat so Tom could extend the pole. The cork stopped, wobbling slightly. 'He's swallowed it,' Whipple said. 'Pull him. Don't jerk, just raise the tip.'

Should'a seen the sucker jump—green and gold and big as a fucking cavalry boot.'"

The Admiral was a big talker, too. Loved to have an audience. As a one-time reporter I was more than happy to be that audience. On one of those sleepless nights when we were both walking on the flight deck, I started the conversation.

"You were a farm boy?" I asked.

The Admiral nodded vigorously. "Tobacco farm down in Southwest Virginia."

"As a boy did you dream of leading a huge armada at sea?"

"As a lad all I wanted was to grow up and fly an aeroplane."

"How'd you get to Annapolis?"

"One of the Virginia senators was a friend of Father's. I hated it as a plebe."

"No early signs of success?"

The Admiral grinned. "Not a fucking sign."

We were walking the flight deck in a brisk stroll, causing crewmen to stop and stare as they realized that the elderly guy in the baseball cap was their Admiral. If actually confronted, they'd salute; otherwise they tended to stand aside and smile. The Admiral, who seemed short of breath, would acknowledge their salutes with a gracious wave. The wind was strong and smelled of the sea and gasoline.

I pursued the questioning. "At the Academy were you a famous quarterback? Or the head of the Corps? Or number one in your class?"

The Admiral's grin returned. "Captain of the swim team, captain of fencing, captain of chess. Nothing heroic."

"Chess? So now you're playing on a bigger scale?"

The old man chuckled. "Guess so and *Amato* was their queen."

He seemed to like that thought. "Their fucking queen."

I hesitated and then took the plunge. "Do you mind if we talk about your son?"

He shook his head and said, "Killed at Pearl Harbor."

"I know, sir. Sorry."

"Lieutenant Commander. Could have been a CAG like Fritz."

We reached the bow, turned with the wind at our back. For several minutes neither of us spoke. Then he said, more cheerfully than I expected. "I wrote his mother. He's buried in a beautiful spot. Flowers, palm trees. Sound of the ocean."

Another silent period, during which we reached the island. He stopped and I figured the walk was over. He changed his mind, lighting a cigarette with his back to the wind. "My wife took it hard. Married to me she knew there was always danger. But she took it hard when Danny was killed." Deep drags on the cigarette. "Great gardener. She's at it all the time. Allergic to sun. Wears my shirts to cover her arms. I got a picture of her holding the shears snipping some buds. Looked like a damn lobster."

After the Admiral went below I stayed on deck. Insomnia. I paced the 200-yard teak deck pleasantly alone, enjoying the smell of the sea, stronger now than gasoline and oil, the smells of the hangar deck. Down there night seemed to have no meaning, as the screaming whine of cutting metal blended with the steady thump of ballpeen hammers.

Above me, as I passed the island, I could detect the whistle of the wind among the many wires, as well as the crackle of radio transmissions. On either side as I walked, the gun tubs held the ship's defensive weapons positioned to fire against attackers.

After the Admiral left, I started to think of apple trees on our farm in the Shenandoah Valley where we lived before my father died. In the spring, if the wind was right, I could smell the trees as soon as I left the main road coming home from school. The shortcut was through the orchard. It was quiet there, except for the bees. I used to wonder how many bees it would take to make the sound of the orchard, like engines humming far away; a million maybe? I loved to watch my father collect honey. My father wore gloves and a wire mask that covered his face and he would go from hive to hive, tall wooden boxes with tiny doors at the base, and lift the top, taking out the wooden honeycombs filled with tiny cells where the honey was stored. Once my grandfather came to visit and gathered the honey without a mask or gloves, allowing the bees to cling to his hands and face without a single sting. When I asked the old man why he wasn't stung, he replied, "They know I'm a friend."

I remembered the orchard in rain when sharp spring winds tore the blossoms from the trees and blew them in my face. I loved the orchard in summer when the small green apples began to form. And I loved it especially in the fall when they turned red and weighed down the branches. I remembered the sound of my father biting a big red apple—crunch!—with the juice running down his chin. I remembered the smell of apples stored in the cool cellar where the cider keg was kept. Halfway around the world, part of a huge battle force, I thought of the peaceful orchard of my boyhood and smiled.

The breeze was strong, carrying—a land smell? Barnyard odors perhaps? Now a rain squall brushed the deck, feeling cool on the face. I thought of rain on the farm after a long dry period. I could see it coming up the road, pelting down like bird shot and washing the reddish dust from roadside weeds. I remembered the sounds rain made at night on the green tin roof of the old house, and the fun I had with my cousin when we dug worms from the barnyard and went fishing for bullheads in the muddy waters of the creek. I remembered my aunt pulling us away from the windows during electrical storms and giving out a little squeak each time lightning slammed into the lightning rod at the barn. I remembered the swimming creatures in the rain barrel from which we took forbidden drinks. Wiping the cool rain from my face, I finally went below in search of sleep.

# Nine

*Young eagles learn:*
*flying is fun.*
*Diving for fish*
*much harder to do.*

Once more with his beloved young fliers, Admiral Ishino held white hachimaki cloths, the ceremonial talisman of ancient Samurai warriors, in his hands. Now that their unit had been named *kamikaze,* the pilots were doubly aware of its significance. Centuries ago an invading fleet of Mongols had been scattered and sunk by a sudden typhoon—a "divine wind," which had saved Japan. Admiral Ishino's pilots would be a new wind that would drive the enemy to his destruction; this was their destiny.

When the hachimaki had been distributed, the pilots helped one another tie the cloths around their heads. The Admiral motioned for his aide to bring the sake and the pilots formed a single line to pass before him. Beneath an unusually clear blue sky appropriately filled with white clouds, the old aviator gave each member of the 200th a small ceremonial drink, followed by a firm handshake. When the Admiral had made his final salute and farewell bow, he climbed back into his Mitsubishi and took off for Tokyo, coughing heavily, but filled with hope.

The Lieutenant Commander gathered his fliers about him. "The first unit will go after transports tomorrow. Second and third will strike carriers. Fourth and fifth in reserve."

Kenishi Osaka was in the first unit. His feelings were mixed. When he thought of the privilege of striking a personal blow in defense of his Emperor and his country, he wanted the band to be playing. Alone on his cot in the dark, he yearned for longer life, yearned to finish his technical studies at college, yearned for a wife and children. He hated the thought that his life would cease, that he would never see another naked woman, or that his erection was for nothing. Was he the only one who thought such cowardly thoughts?

Kasu was also awake. Osaka could hear the springs squeak as he turned restlessly. Finally Osaka reached over and tapped him on the shoulder.

"You all right?"

"Fine. You?"

He didn't sound fine. Osaka leaned closer. "Scared?"

"Certainly not. What kind of question is that?"

"It's natural to worry."

"Who's worried?"

"I am."

"That's your problem. I'm excited."

"Good for you."

"I'm going to sink a ship for the Emperor."

"If you're lucky."

"The Emperor will bring me luck. He will find the ship."

Osaka wondered if he believed that.

Nearby, Baso continued to feed on his dream. Tomorrow would be the day. Smiling, he continued to replay the filmstrip of his imaginary attack.

The long night passed slowly, with water whispering in the downspouts and sleepy birds murmuring in the safety of the trees.

Dawn at last. Hot tea. Special breakfast—gruel and rice. Intelligence briefing. Crisp. Business-like. "Anti-aircraft range so many meters." So many ships reported. So far away. Such and such coordinates—quite easy as if printed on the sea in large numerals. "Be sure to arm your bomb when the enemy is sighted. It's very unhealthy to arm them beforehand—in case you return to the field."

No smiles. The Admiral can talk that way. Not a nasty little intelligence fellow they'd never seen.

Now they stood together for the last time. All hands were nervous and jumpy. Even the fourth and fifth units in reserve. Handshakes. Small jokes. Will they really meet in the Emperor's garden? Say so anyway. Engines sputtered. Exhaust smoke belched.

The Lieutenant Commander took Ensign Osaka aside at the last minute. "You will lead unit one. You will *not* dive. Someone must return and report what happens. You can find the enemy for the others. You are a good flier."

When the Ensign started to protest, the Lieutenant Commander said, "That's an order, Ensign. Don't worry. Your time will come soon enough."

Stunned, Osaka walked over to the five pilots of unit one. Without looking at them he said, "I am to find the target and report your success. Not dive."

After a moment, Baso said, "Tough luck."

Osaka looked at him quickly, but there was no way to tell whether the remark was sarcasm or genuine regret. Osaka began to jog toward his plane, calling back, "Stay close. If you don't see a target, return to base. Be sure you're not armed!"

Yesterday's fair weather had gone. Rain was back. Clouds were back. The islands and sun below have disappeared in skim milk. Soon the six planes were in heavy cloud. As they emerged one was missing. Nowhere in sight. Will he catch up? Has he lost power and crashed? Osaka studied his chart. Two small islands, with a curving channel leading to a large bay. That would be Balacat Bay. But where were the transports? Where was shipping of any kind? That little cockroach from intelligence had been so sure as if he had placed the ships there himself.

Osaka dropped down 1,000 feet to make sure. Only four planes followed. The cloud had eaten the other plane. No sign. Nothing on the radio. Just silence.

Osaka made a low sweep over the area. No doubt about it. Everything checked. But no bloody transports. No fucking carriers. The Ensign signalled "return to base" and began climbing as he turned his chart around. Halfway home his wingman developed engine trouble. Running rough. Flames. Smoke. The last he saw of him he was spiralling down to an open field surrounded by rice paddies.

Strong headwinds pushed down from the north as the fighters struggled to reach base. About 30 miles from home Osaka signalled "jettison bombs" and the trio of remaining aircraft dropped down for a clear view of empty sea and sent the 250-pound explosives tumbling into the water.

Osaka checked his chart, headed northeast just below the overcast. He managed to find the field, though a storm was in progress. Yanking off his helmet, he ran through deep puddles to the operations office where the Lieutenant Commander was waiting. The other two pilots stumbled in, dripping water. One of them was Kasu; the other was Baso. The Commander knew from their expressions the mission had failed. Wrong intelligence. Faulty aircraft. He was glad the Admiral was in Tokyo.

In fact the Admiral was not in Tokyo.

Upon leaving their camp the Admiral had mixed feelings; pride in the young fliers and their bravery; sorrow over the prospect of their imminent death. He took his farewell from them all lined up before him as they'd done on his arrival. He didn't trust himself to address them, so he saluted them as a unit, climbed into his Mitsubishi aircraft, took the copilot seat and said, "Let's go." His aide remained behind to work on tactics. The Admiral noticed that the formation of fliers held together until he had become airborne and returned over the field. On some obscure command every man in formation raised his hand in a farewell gesture, bringing tears to the Admiral's eyes.

He sat, lost in thought, as the small passenger plane flew north over the islands, through thick clouds, past an occasional unidentifiable coastal ship. After thirty minutes flying he was almost asleep when a tracer bullet zipped past the wing. He turned and saw an American fighter diving on them. There was no escape, unless a cloud formation should appear. He looked down; they were over an island. Noticing that his pilot was sitting on a parachute the Admiral said in firm tones, "Listen to me. Bail out."

"But Admiral—"

"No time to argue. Go. He won't shoot you in midair. Get out."

"Sir, I cannot abandon—"

"I'm a pilot. I'll be okay. Jump!"

The tracers were being followed by .50 calibers cutting across the wing. The big blue plane was circling and descending.

"Admiral, I refuse—"

The Admiral reached over, with surprising strength, yanked the pilot out of his seat and shoved him backwards into the seating area. Then he grabbed the parachute on which the pilot had been seated. "Strap this on and get out."

His commands had the force of physical blows. The pilot quickly shrugged into the parachute harness and ran to the door where he hesitated.

"Jump!" the old man called. "Out of the plane. Jump! Jump!"

The pilot said something the Admiral couldn't hear. Then he opened the door, looked once more towards the Admiral, and tumbled forward. Just in time. The F6F zoomed down and sprayed .50 caliber rounds everywhere, including where the reluctant pilot had been. The Admiral tried to stabilize the plane. Too bad he had no guns to fight back with. As the American fighter returned, the Admiral pushed the damaged aircraft into a left hand dive, causing the bullets to go astray. Then he smelled smoke from an earlier run and realized the end was near. Too bad he couldn't make it more costly. The Navy fighter turned and dove for the last time. The Admiral caught sight of the parachute and smiled a second before the plane exploded, almost close enough to engulf the American fighter—but not quite.

# Ten

The Captain was a chess player, far better than I, but always eager for a game. He played chess the way he ran his ship, briskly, courageously, in relentless pursuit of his opponent. As we all know, chess is not a chatty game; nor was the Captain by nature very talkative compared with the Admiral, for instance; yet, so confident was he when playing with me, that he became positively garrulous. A night I recall most clearly began pleasantly, for him, with the early capture of my queen, which seemed to unlock something in him that took him back to Philadelphia in the days before he went to Annapolis.

Against a background of engines starting, distant metal screeching and the ever-present sound of the waves, we sat in his sea cabin drinking Cokes. "I used to play tennis with my father. He was a tall fellow—like you—who had a terrific serve. I had never beaten him. We ended up playing for club championship. To my surprise a very close game. I didn't know whether this meant Dad was slipping or I had suddenly climbed up a 'match.'" He chuckled. He paused, moved a black bishop, and smiled; his mind still in the past. "Our game got to be embarrassing—with lots of club people suddenly taking an interest. I remember thinking, 'Should I really be doing this to my father in public?' And then he'd send one of those cannonball serves my way and I'd forget my misgivings. When things got down to break point I was going after him as if he were something to be exterminated. I guess I tried too hard. Dad won four points in a row and I was whipped. Afterwards, he seemed so happy I was glad it turned out that way. Checkmate."

I looked at the chessboard in dismay. But there it was. My king, threatened, had no place to go. The Captain chuckled. It was early evening. We could smell the sea, the gasoline, and down below somebody was cooking tomorrow's bread.

"What was your father's occupation?" I asked.

"Naval officer," McCord said. "Vice Admiral."

I whistled. "Was it tough growing up with an Admiral?"

"Not really. When he was home we enjoyed him as a father. You might say he didn't run a very tight ship at home."

"When he was home? Was he gone a lot?"

He nodded. "Commanded the Atlantic Fleet for a while. A full-time job, believe me."

"How about Dan Duncan? Did they cross paths?"

"He was gunnery officer on Dad's cruiser."

McCord smiled. "He came up and told me Dad was a tough cookie. I guess he's trying to copy my old man."

In our next chess session the Captain spoke again of his father. I had kept his attention for longer than usual with a more aggressive gambit or two. When he thought he had blunted the main thrust of my attack, he brought two Cokes from his mini-refrigerator and offered me one. He took a gurgling gulp and wiped his mouth with the back of his hand. "Did I tell you my father was once Superintendent of the Naval Academy?"

"When was that?"

"Unfortunately, during two of my four years."

"Wow! No chance to beat him at tennis under those circumstances?"

"No chance at all. As a plebe I could hardly breathe in his official presence."

"Any problems?"

"One or two."

"Classified?"

He chuckled and moved a knight. "Not exactly. There was a problem about a Sweet Briar girl after a dance that came close. But we managed to get her out of the window in time and I drove her to her inn. Got away with that one. But I did end up in his office on a more serious occasion. We had a history exam and my instructor accused me of cheating. It seems he found my paper was word-for-word with what had been in the text—plus his lecture. So there I am facing my father and this angry instructor. My father had already guessed what had happened, but he played the role of superintendent for all it was worth. 'You are accused of cheating, McCord. What do you have to say?'

"'Not guilty, sir.'

"'Have you any proof?'

"'Yes, sir. I have a good memory.'

"The instructor spoke up, 'Nobody can recall a text and a lecture *verbatim*. Absolutely verbatim.'

"Hiding his smile, my father said, 'There's one way to find out. McCord?'

"I don't know where it came from but I had this damn gift of photographic memory. And Dad knew it. We'd kidded about it for years. I cleared my throat and rattled off names, dates etc., as if I were reading them.

"After about five minutes the instructor threw up his hands. 'All right, all right, you win, young man... I regret this, Admiral. My apology to all.'

"Still with a straight face, Dad said, 'Next time be sure of your facts before you accuse someone of cheating.'

"'Aye, sir.'" The Captain laughed.

Hearing the story, I felt sorry for the poor instructor.

"Checkmate," the Captain said, smiling.

"Damn," I said.

I was on the main bridge when Captain McCord took a blinker message from the destroyer *Sherman*, plane guard to *Sussex* : "Ensign Martinez urgently requests high line transfer to you soonest. Willing to attempt despite sea condition if you approve. Martinez sustained cracked rib in ditching, but insists he's okay to make crossing. You're welcome to him. Jenkins."

McCord picked up the phone on the bridge and called XO. "The can wants to send us a flier on the high line. Can we do it this late and in this sea?"

I could imagine the XO saying, "It won't be an easy ride."

"It's one of our kids who ditched last night. Got a busted rib in the bargain. Thing is: Can we do it?"

"Yes, sir. We can do it. If we hurry."

"Good. Let's move."

The Captain sent a return blinker message. "Approved. Process immediately. Warn Martinez no picnic. McCord."

We heard the gun boom and watched the line whistle between the ships, watched the rigging take place, saw the small figure in oilskins emerge from a door of the destroyer and then become surrounded by a group who helped him into the bosun's chair. The seas were cresting with wind-blown tops as the line tightened and the bosun's chair swung away from the destroyer and began its slow progress to the carrier.

I knew how the kid felt out there, suspended above the big waves. He was probably sorry he'd raised such a stink to get transferred. His rib certainly ached and now he might be seasick in front of the crew of both ships who stood at the rail like audiences watching a circus acrobat. I could imagine him thinking, "Holy Mother, I'm a goner. Here comes the whole fucking ocean... " The wind-driven top of a wave slapped against him. "Fuck you!" he screamed at the ocean in fury, wiping the salt water from his face. It looked as if having failed to get him the night before, the Pacific was reaching out to swallow him again. For some reason his dousing seemed to amuse the crew lined up on the carrier. They cheered merrily. "Fuck you, too!" Marty shouted, shaking his fist and producing more cheers. One more wave nipped at his feet before he reached the other side, where a dozen hands were ready to pull him aboard. "Thanks, fellas."

Cheers. "Welcome home," somebody said.

When Martinez reached the carrier I steered him to Dr. Swartz who took x-rays and taped him up. Martinez stuck his head in afterwards and I invited him to have a seat.

"That was close," he said, rolling his eyes.

"Are you fit to fly," I asked. "Affirmative decision?"

He nodded. "Not at first. He knew it was painful and said I shouldn't be in the plane on a long flight maybe five to six hours there and back to reach the battleship. I said I don't care about discomfort. Flying with the group this time would be the greatest thing I'd ever done. He said I was not 'broken just sprained' but it would be extremely painful and I was crazy to want to do this. I smiled at him and said 'Everybody in my family says that.' So I'm crazy. But Commander Rawlings needs a crazy man if he can fly an F6F. That's me, *loco amigo.*"

In the wardroom which smelled of coffee and freshly baked bread, Rawlings found a seat in the midst of the fighter pilots and looked around. They seemed subdued. "How's it going, gentlemen?" he asked, sounding more cheerful than he felt.

"Okay, Skipper," somebody said, without enthusiasm.

"Dandy," another said, equally flat.

The ship's motion tilted the level of water in the glasses.

"What's eating you fellows?" Fritz asked. "Seasick?"

"What about the fucking battleship?" somebody asked. "Where the hell is it?"

"They'll find her," Fritz said. "There's a big search under way. We'll get our shot."

This was the first time Rawlings had detected a morale problem. He had seen this one coming. They'd been yanked off one strike and sent off on another with little rest. They'd come up empty and then had a hairy night landing with very little fuel. He was also aware that each pilot knew that an attack on Japanese battleships was a bitch and that nobody in the Navy had done a damn thing against those monsters, though plenty of guys had died trying.

Martinez entered the wardroom and found a seat across from Rawlings, who was surprised to see him. His entrance silenced the group. "Hullo," Marty said, realizing he had become the center of attention and hating it.

"How's the rib?" Rawlings asked.

"Not too bad," Marty said, reaching for his napkin.

"That's one easy way to get a Purple Heart," Stone said at the end of the table. There was a mean little laugh, in which Rawlings did not join. Marty could feel his face getting red. Rawlings spoke up, "How many of you guys would turn down R and R in Hawaii?"

"Nobody turns down R and R, Commander."

"Marty just did."

"Guy's nuts. I knew it all along."

Marty wanted to get up and leave, but he knew what Rawlings was trying to do and leaving would be very bad.

"So you're going to stay aboard the dear old *Sussex*?" somebody asked from the end of the table.

Marty said, "That's right."

"Doing what?" Stone asked, creating an acid silence. I wanted to say, "One more crack like that and I'll knock your teeth out," but you don't fight smaller men especially when it might be your teeth that get knocked out.

Rawlings slammed down his spoon. "All right, guys, let's get something straight." His tone was icy. "Marty ran out of gas last night. Some of you did too, but lucked out. He requested permission to come aboard. But there was a fire and he was told to ditch. He did so. Damn near drowned. He was picked up by the can."

Marty could hold it no longer. In an angry voice he said, "Not only did he run out of fuel, gentlemen, he ran out of guts, nerve, courage, and balls—take your pick. In other words he fucked up. You heard him."

"Hold it, Marty."

"Excuse me, Commander. Not quite through." He turned to Stone, "I don't blame you for asking what I'd be doing aboard this ship. I've been asking myself the same question. 'Do you belong in a fighter squadron, Martinez'? I said. 'Does anybody want to fly with a guy who fucked up in the air with the whole squadron listening'?"

Rawlings leaned forward, demanding attention. "All right, Marty. Now it's my turn." He paused and looked at his fliers. Some of them had been with him at Midway, some in the Mariannas shoot. Some were almost as new as Marty. They were neither better nor worse than any other squadron; only they were his and they tried his patience sometimes. "I'm returning Martinez to duty," he said, in a way that ended further comment. "Not because I feel sorry for him. Not because everybody deserves a second chance. None of that bullshit. He's a trained pilot who hit the panic button as we all do sooner or later, and I need him. Just as I need every one of you bastards."

To relieve the obvious tension, Terry Vernon stood up and said "especially me." Everybody laughed.

Later Fritz and I chatted in his cabin. He was too wound up to sleep. I could have used a little shut-eye but Fritz had a greater need. For the first time after all the months since we'd sailed without his wife on the dock in San Diego, Fritz seemed anxious to talk.

I'd been aware of the situation that had ended with Fritz's divorce. After our first tour of duty the Air Group had returned to San Diego and Fritz had undertaken to visit the widows of the four guys we'd lost in the Mariannas. One of the widows was a tall blonde named Mary Lee Douglas whose husband, Chip Douglas, had gone down in flames on our final mission aboard the *Princeton*.

When we sailed aboard *Sussex*, I missed the usual slim brunette waving beside the stationwagon on the San Diego dock—Mrs. Rawlings. Fritz seemed depressed as we stood together on the stern of *Sussex* when she headed back to war.

"Good leave?" Fritz said.

"Great. How about you?"

"Lousy."

At that moment he wasn't ready. Now, with the attack on the battleship looming, he seemed to want to tell me what happened.

He waited a while before he brought up the subject. "You met Chip's widow? So you know she's a knockout. First time I went there, I stayed ten minutes. Not even a Coke. Just enough time for me to describe what a good flier Chip was. 'Thanks for coming. You've been so kind. Chip always adored you.' That kind of talk."

I'd met Mary Lee Douglas. Molasses poured over corn cakes. Fritz continued, "Next time it was, 'You got time to share a beer with a lonely widow?'"

"Why not?" I said.

"Everybody could see it coming—except me. Sure enough, third visit dry martinis and steak dinner for 'the sailor' all that crap. Plus a good night kiss that shoulda told me to get the hell outa there. You can guess the rest. Before I know what the hell is happening, we're having an affair and Lucy's on the warpath. Before I know it I'm getting ultimatums and—shit—I don't love that fucking Douglas woman but she has busted up my marriage. Am I a fucking idiot or what?"

I had no answer to that.

Like many Virginia graduates I treasure the memory of the Rotunda, Jefferson's half-scale replica of Rome's Pantheon. Maggie's latest letter had contained a winter photo of the Rotunda rising in quiet majesty above a hushed snowy Lawn. I'd taped it to the bulkhead, like Martinez' Jesus, and enjoyed its cool, peaceful permanence. I remembered my year on the Lawn in the same room that my grandfather had. I remembered waking up to snow and selecting my thick wool robe to make the morning dash along the arcades to the showers. Sweating in my bunk half a world away, I savored the memory of winter at the University, of a snowball fight with student neighbors. Later, half asleep, I could almost smell the woodsmoke of my fireplace, could clearly see the kindling stacked outside my door.

Where has all the Latin gone, so charmingly taught by Professors Alexander and Linwood Lehman? Four years of well-taught Latin and all that's left is my ability to greet someone on the verge of my death, *Morituri te Salutamus.* At least I'll have company. I yearned to hear once more the sharp comments of my creative English professor, Armistead Gordon, who could cut down a young writer's flowery words as if he were mowing grass on a grave.

I wondered what had happened to the University's hostess, a rare patrician lady who poured tea, gave quiet pragmatic advice—and had a shapely daughter. How I'd love to see them again! The real world had become more than I had bargained for. Now I needed dreams of yesterday.

I remembered a special snowy day in New York. I was a $15-a-week office boy who had just gotten a raise to $20 and we lived in a one-room apartment on 8th Street. That evening after work I returned home by subway, five cents, waited for the trolley to pass on 8th Street. Crossed over slipping and sliding, climbed the dark stairs over the Japanese restaurant, and found a note on the door. "You don't live here anymore. Try 26 West 9th."

I couldn't believe my eyes. Trudging through the snow I hustled around the corner. I found all our modest possessions in a new apartment with two rooms, a fire burning in a small fireplace and dinner in the oven! Proudly, she told me she'd found the apartment, raced "to find a drayman with horse," miraculously had done so and persuaded him to carry bed, chairs, dresser downstairs and drive them—in the falling snow—to number 26. Her eyes were shining and she was chuckling as she related her triumph. We then ate the casserole and washed the dishes, put pillows on the floor, turned out the lights, and lay in front of the fire, savoring our good fortune.

As my recollections traveled a snowy path I also remembered a winter railroad trip to California Maggie and I made years later. We had a delightful relaxed three days in the compartment, watching the country roll by, feeling wickedly isolated. On our return she suggested that we detour past Sun Valley. Without ski clothing, she nevertheless decided to ride the ski lift to the top. Since I had no coat (why take one to California?) I put on *two* suits and she—as nonchalant as an Olympic champion—wrapped herself in her fur coat and rode up with correctly dressed skiers to the top of the mountain, passing through snow on the way. Drinking a hot toddy in the tavern at the top she was happy as a lark, gathering about herself a group of young people amused by her audacity. Meanwhile, feeling like a Martian businessman who'd fallen out of the sky, I enjoyed her truimph and tried unsuccessfully to become invisible.

# Eleven

*First blood for
the young warriors.
Fortune smiles, though
Somewhat sadly.*

Having taken aboard all survivors of the destroyer, *Amato* headed once again for the Philippines where the Allies—according to dispatches—were coming ashore at Leyte Gulf. On her bridge, wet from the spray and drizzle, Captain Osaka was scanning the western horizon. The smell of land was strong. The wind bore the familiar odors of wet grass and vegetation, with a trace of barnyard. He thought of his father's farm where the coming of fall was a busy time for the family. A rewarding and happy time when the boys worked the fields with the peasants and the barns were full of sweet-smelling crops. As the Captain wiped the moisture from his glasses he thought of the destroyer Captain who had saved his life—and the life of God knows how many *Amato* sailors. A blinker message from the picket destroyer. "Search plane reports small task force including transports. Two escort carriers. Three destroyers. Dead ahead."

At last, a chance to fight again. The Captain called for General Quarters and spoke to his helmsman. "Holding at flank speed, Mr. Samuri?"

"Aye, sir. Holding at flank."

"Very well. Steady as she goes."

The great ship continued to surge forward through a restless sea. Her wake glowed with white foam and her flanking vessels turned up their screws in anticipation of combat.

In the rare circumstance of having a son aboard his ship Captain

Osaka saw no harm in bending a few rules. He ordered Miro to report to the bridge as officer of the day and enjoyed the boy's presence on the bridge while *Amato* moved into a battle zone. As if they were father and son at home, they talked of life on the farm when Miro was a boy and more on his post-war career. As in their first talk together aboard the *Amato*, the father was not encouraging on the subject of a naval career. This was hard for Miro to accept, since he had spent much of his short life wanting to emulate his father. On that subject Captain Osaka was firm, "Don't get your heart set on the Navy. I don't think there will be such a thing."

"How can an island nation not have a navy?" the boy asked.

"Because the Americans will not permit it. They will never forgive Pearl Harbor. Never."

Twenty miles westward unit one of the special attack force was launched into its second venture. Leading the six planes, as before, was Ensign Osaka, now more determined than ever to find a target and guide his unit to a significant strike. He had adjusted to the role of pathfinder and reporting officer. At first it seemed to compromise his decision to die for his country, but he had been assured that his time would come; meanwhile, he could make a greater contribution by leading less skilled men to distant targets.

Again, they were flying through thick wet clouds. He signalled for them to close ranks and tighten up the formation. Each time they broke out of a cloud into the sunshine he checked to make sure everybody was present. He studied the chart with satisfaction. Again he was right on track. He thought: "Let's hope the intelligence fellow had better information this time." Through the next break in the clouds Osaka found what he was looking for: two transports, three destroyers and— his pulse quickened—a pair of escort carriers. Now that the enemy was in sight his job was finished, but the temptation to make the first dive was strong. He put it out of his mind and signalled the assignments: one to each transport, two for each carrier. He pulled away, saluting his unit, feeling a sudden catch in his throat. In less than five minutes they would all be dead. Pray that it's worth the cost. He climbed above anti-aircraft range and circled back to observe results.

Baso's dream was about to become a reality. He was the first to push over. He headed for one of the carriers. Anti-aircraft bursts suddenly bloomed nearby. They seemed to be part of the scene. Their black smoke, lingering in the air, gave him reference points and a sense of speed. The escort carrier was coming up fast. She was full of guns. A beautiful target. So many men running. She's turning, trying to get away from me.

You cannot escape. He pressed the button of his machine guns and watched the tracers hit the water and then the deck. He didn't want his dive to be over so quickly. Only another second or two left. Which target area? The island. Hit the island and kill the captain. Yelling at the top of his voice, Baso did just that.

The destroyers had now begun shooting. The second pilot was attacking a transport. Black flowers were blooming around the other four divers as they descended on the carriers in hurtling pairs. All ships were in high speed evasive maneuvers, cutting white circles in the green water. Two Combat Air Patrol aircraft tried to intercept, but the Japanese had the advantage of surprise and speed. Almost simultaneously all attacking planes struck their targets and exploded. Flames rose from each allied ship. Osaka shouted "Banzai." Baso was gone. They all were gone. All six gone where? Blown to bits by bomb fragments? Burning in gasoline? Kasu had flown his plane into a forward elevator shaft and landed among gassing aircraft. A dead hero now amid enemy dead and dying. Baso, too, smashed against the island. Were they now in the Emperor's garden? Or were they just plain dead? Fighting back tears, Osaka turned north toward Cebu to carry the good news.

His father in *Amato's* darkened fire control room studied the screen where the escort carriers were electronically trapped in green symbols.
"Fire."
The huge shell screamed across the nine miles of open water and struck the *Tampa Bay*, bursting into her engine room and blowing a huge hole below the water line. Her boiler-room crew died instantly. The escort carrier—already in flames—took on water fast and began to list. A second shell from *Amato* was a semi-armor piercing shot triggered by the carrier's thin hull that almost reached the opposite hull before it exploded. The third landed on the forecastle and obliterated the crews quarters. *Tampa Bay's* Captain, listening to his damage control reports, shook his fist at the sky. His Exec had been killed and more than one hundred of his people were dead. The diving plane had gone into the hangar deck where many were gassing up. Another had hit the bridge. "Fucking kamikazes! Now some sonofabitch in a battlewagon thinks we're a sitting duck. Let's get the fuck out of here. This is the Captain speaking—abandon ship! Abandon ship!"

Three planes that had taken off before the attack on *Tampa Bay* formed up and flew toward *Amato* like angry wasps. The Captain had been expecting them. His ship was already at G.Q.; no need for further alarms. Anti-aircraft puffs quickly bloomed in the enemy's path. One F6F was hit. Immediately it tumbled out of formation, trailing smoke all the way to the water. Halfway down, the pilot bailed out and swung about the fleet in a creamy parachute. A second plane swooped down on *Amato*, strafing left and right. Two gunners fell from their posts, apparently hit by .50 calibers. The third Hellcat dropped a small bomb near the anchor locker where it blew up without incident. All other enemy aircraft were confined to their carriers where the wooden decks were burning.

Ensign Osaka stood in front of the Lieutenant Commander's desk while the Commander talked on the phone. The Commander's voice was exultant as he told the Admiral of the unit's first success. When he finished, he offered his hand to the Ensign. "The High Command's compliments."

Osaka was embarrassed. He knew where the compliments should be going.

Why not "The Admiral's compliments?"

The question stuck in the back of his mind. He wanted the Admiral to know. In this case he wanted the Admiral to know about Baso and Kasu. He hated the false credit. Next day the word came through; the Admiral was dead. Ken felt as if somebody had hit him in the stomach. He had felt the same way when his grandfather had died. Sorrow and then anger. No anger with his grandfather but the same sudden loneliness, the knowledge that he'd never see the old man again. When he heard the Admiral's unarmed plane had been shot down, that produced the anger. He owed the Americans one. Now he had the motivation. With this single criminal act they had made an enemy they'd be sorry to have before he was through.

# Twelve

The OOD and I were chatting when Admiral Duncan arrived, out of breath. It must have been close to midnight. I couldn't sleep down below and the fresh air felt good. The Admiral accepted a cup of coffee and said, "You should be in the sack, Mason. What's got you up here?"

"Not much of a sleeper, Admiral."

I followed him out to the wing of the bridge. He looked up at the stars. "Don't they seem close out here?"

"Yes, sir."

He pointed, "There's old Dog Star, Sirius. God, it looks close enough to reach up and unscrew it like a light bulb."

He stared at the sky for a few minutes. "Wouldn't it have been great to navigate like the Polynesians? To sail thousands of miles across the Pacific and make a landfall on an island no bigger than a fly speck on a map."

Below on the windy flight deck the crews were spotting aircraft—; elevators lifting them, tractors pulling them in place. The Admiral watched, as the ship prepared for battle. Armor-piercing bombs, rockets and torpedoes were hauled to the waiting planes. The TBMs, pregnant with torpedoes, came last. Then the activity stopped and the flight deck was packed for take-off with fighters first, then bombers, then torpeckers. Below us nearly 3,000 men slept or prepared for the coming day. I thought about the guys in the engine room. Though the aircraft were armed and ready and the pilots were sleeping, the engine room knew neither night nor day. I imagined them down there in full stride with the spinning turbines, burning fuel, heating boilers—half-naked bunch watching gauges, oiling bearings, adjusting pressures.

The Admiral suddenly stepped to the door and beckoned to the Duty Officer manning flag plot. The Lieutenant saluted and came over. The Admiral pointed. "See the tractor?"

"Yes, Admiral."

"I want to talk to the driver."

After a moment of hesitation, the Lieutenant nodded and picked up a phone. The Admiral stepped outside and resumed his study of the stars. In less than ten minutes, the Lieutenant opened the door and said, "He's here, sir."

"Send him in."

A young sailor, looking petrified, stepped out of the bridge and saluted. "Nevitt, sir, Seaman First Class."

The Admiral smiled and stuck out his hand.

"Relax, son. I'm not going to bite you."

Nevitt shook the Admiral's firm hand. "And this is Lieutenant Mason."

I shook his chilly hand. The boy tried to return the Admiral's smile, but it was a strain. The old man turned and leaned on the rail, facing forward. "I was watching you, Nevitt. You run that yellow John Deere?"

"Yes, sir." He stood frozen, holding his cap in both hands.

"Like the work?"

"Yes, sir. I drove a tractor before."

"Where?"

"Missouri, sir."

"Farm boy?"

"Yes, sir."

"How do you like the Navy?"

Nevitt's voice strengthened, "I like it Admiral, sir. But I'd rather be home."

"Me too, Nevitt. Me too."

Nevitt was still waiting for the blow to fall. Why had a *three-star-Admiral* sent for him. Holy cow!

I felt sorry for him.

"I grew up on a tobacco farm in southern Virginia," the Admiral said.

"No kidding? I mean, yes, sir."

The idea of an Admiral ever being anywhere but at sea seemed hard to grasp.

"We had an old tractor that was always breaking down." Duncan said.

"Ours too," Nevitt said in amazement, "as if some days it didn't want to work."

He began to relax a little.

"What do you miss the most?" The Admiral offered him a cigarette. He shook his head. "Don't smoke, sir."

The question took Nevitt by surprise.

"Well, sir, my dog I guess. Though I wouldn't like the folks to hear me say that. I miss old Red."

"I can understand that," the Admiral said. "I missed my dog for years."

In the pause that followed the ship took a big wave, slowed, then pushed on. In a machine shop on the hangar deck a whining saw cut into metal. A steady roar outlasted the scream; the deep roar of the stacks burning up oily exhaust from the engines and pouring smoke across the stars like a veil.

The Admiral became aware of the farm boy waiting to learn why he'd been summoned. The old man put a hand on Nevitt's shoulder.

"I just wanted you to know that the people running this ship appreciate what you and others are doing. We're not all sonsofbitches in spite of what you hear."

"Oh, no, sir!" Nevitt said.

"You'll see that old dog before too long, Nevitt. I promise you. We're going to beat the Japanese and then everybody will go home."

"That'll be fine, sir."

"Goodnight."

"Goodnight, Admiral, sir. I'm sure glad to meet you."

"Thanks."

Nevitt clamped his hat back on and saluted smartly.

Watching him go, the old man shook his head. "How can anyone be that young?"

I was surprised by the Admiral. I knew he was a great talker who needed an audience; but it never occurred to me that, in order to get his mind off the impending battle, and its loss of life, he'd want to talk about his son again. I'm not sure just what got him started; it might have been a letter from his wife acknowledging his description of where Danny was buried. The sea was lumpy, but the ship took the swells easily and all was quiet; stars were bright. The two of us leaned against the railing, facing forward, one of the better moments of Navy life for me.

"Danny was a natural athlete, natural leader. Captain of his high school baseball team. Quarterback at Annapolis. Ran like a deer."

The old man paused, savoring the picture of his boy in the sunny fields of memory. "I was so proud the day he beat Army. It was in Philadelphia and snowing like hell but we didn't care—Emma and I. Danny was all over the field. Scored three touchdowns. When he graduated we waited to see which way he was going. At first, it looked like submarines—that's where the challenges were, the excitement. Then he got bitten by the flying bug and off he went to Jacksonville."

I said, "I know that bug, sir."

"Yes, of course. Well anyway, when he gets his wings he decides on torpeckers and he's on a flattop in the Med for a while. As a matter of fact during my tour of duty over there, I saw him for a weekend leave. Then he gets transferred to Hawaii. Now he had a family. Pretty little wife and son." The Admiral stopped. Comes the hard part.

In a change of tone, he went on. "Morning of the attack Danny was in the hangar. Ran out and tried to get a fighter off the ground. Didn't make it."

There didn't seem to be anything for me to say.

He continued, "Some people today are saying the Japanese attack was 'brilliantly executed. A feat of deception and execution without parallel.'" The gravel surged into his voice. "I say the Japs will be sorry they ever left home before we're through with them. They killed my son. I'm going to kill ten thousand of theirs." His voice broke and I was glad we were standing in darkness. His remarks embarrassed me—as they probably embarrassed him, once said. Abruptly he decided to let the sea wind and the darkness take over—fortunately.

Then he changed the subject—to Admiral Spruance. "Fellow had never commanded an air group or a carrier before he took over from Halsey." Halsey had been hospitalized at Pearl with a skin infection before Midway. "Spruance didn't get much help from land-based Army, Marines defending Midway. Everybody took to the skies but nobody's bombs hit a fucking thing. Then our carrier-based boys got lucky and we knocked off those Jap carriers, a lovely sight! When the Jap high command realized what had happened they pulled their battleships and heavy cruisers back and waited for the Americans to follow up their victory—which was something almost every American commander would have done. But not Spruance. So the Japs with all that firepower are setting out there saying to themselves, 'The Americans will follow their victory by pursuing our fleet. And when they do we will blow them away, eat them alive.' A logical and reasonable position, but they didn't know Spruance. Though he had a lot of pressure from his staff to do just that, he was too smart to risk all we had left by doing the obvious. Good man—Spruance."

He paused and yawned mightily.

"Good night, Mike. Big day tomorrow."

"Yes, sir. Good night, Admiral."

Again I was too tired to sleep. I lay fully dressed on my bunk, trying to forget the ship, the war, the aching loneliness. As I gradually relaxed, my mind went back to winter mornings after my father's death when we lived across the Potomac from Washington and I attended Western High School in Georgetown. Sometimes I took the bus, sometimes the streetcar. I preferred the trolley because it went faster and seemed to have a spirit of its own. It bounced and swayed, clanging its bell and hooting as it sped downhill past Fort Myer through Virginia countryside to Rosslyn. In the winter the trolley pole skipped along the overhead wire and showered sparks when the ice broke the connection. From Rosslyn I marched across Key Bridge, fighting the wind. Despite the cold, I never failed to get a kick out of the view. Upriver the snow-covered Three Sisters Islands reminded me of the summer day when my mother and I had watched my father swim across the river, touching the islands on the way. Downstream the island that became Roosevelt Island, reminded me of the first smallmouth bass I caught with my father near its weedy shore. Once across, I climbed the long hill to school, lugging my books and losing my breath as I raced against the opening bell.

With me many mornings was my first girl, Helen Middlebury, a small, blue-eyed girl with silky blonde hair, a pouting lower lip, and growing causes for excitement hidden beneath her blouse. Helen irritated me because she always finished her homework, always had the written assignment neatly done, always knew what Caesar was up to in his tedious Gallic Wars. I had every intention of marrying Helen until she went to an Annapolis hop and fell in love. As best man in their wedding, standing at the chapel, I had watched Helen come up the aisle, petite and beautiful in her white gown, and cursed myself for not asking her first.

I finally got up, took a shower, and fell into bed, where I dreamed of snow. I was eight years old and was riding my Flexible Flyer down the hill behind Fort Myer and the streetcar at the foot of the hill was pulling blue sparks off the icy trolley wire.

# Thirteen

*Massive gray presence.*
*How many enemies to*
*bring down the elephant?*

*Amato's* new mission was a stunning surprise: make the ship the prime target at Okinawa in order to draw off enemy aircraft and allow the Special Attack Force to strike American carriers in suicide dives with a minimum of air cover. Before she left her mooring, the assignment was abundantly clear in orders from the General Staff. Half capacity fuel. No round trip this time. The one-way ticket to nowhere.

In his sea cabin Captain Osaka could hear the great pumps working as he wrote his wife:

Dearest Kei,
    In their infinite wisdom our superiors in Tokyo have decided that the battleship is no longer a primary naval weapon. She has now become an attractive target for enemy aircraft. We leave tonight on our last voyage, which will probably be over by the time this is in your hands.
    I don't expect to survive. In the ancient tradition the captain goes down with his ship. As a matter of pride, how could I swim away when my men are drowning?
    You have been an excellent wife. I thank you for your good humor, for our sons, for the serenity of our home, for the charms of our love-making.
    Please don't grieve uselessly. We knew from the start that a sailor's life was full of risk. Few men in our armed forces are really counting on survival. The country's survival is what's important.

Goodbye, my dear wife. I pray for you and the boys. Miro will be with you soon. He needs your help.
Kato


When he finished the letter, Captain Osaka sent for his son. He waited for the boy in his sea cabin off the main bridge. Miro came quickly, saluted, stood at attention. The Captain smiled and told him to shut the door, which he did. And, "Relax," which he did.

"I'm transferring you off this ship," the Captain said.

"But, sir, I was hoping—"

"Never mind. You have leave coming anyway. And when you come back—"

"Excuse me, Father, sir. But is there any way this can be changed? I don't mean to take advantage of kinship, but you have thousands of men aboard. Isn't there a place for an ensign with destroyer experience?"

His voice faltered; his father heaved a sigh, put an arm across the boy's shoulders.

"Listen to me, Miro. This ship has been ordered to Okinawa. Do you know why? As a target for American planes. The High Command has decided that if we are near enough to their carrier fleet she will draw their aircraft and our land-based planes can attack their carriers against weak defenses."

The enormity of what he was hearing silenced the young officer. To him *Amato* was indestructible, the very essence of power at sea. How could his father be accepting such orders so calmly. Was there no appeal? The Captain shrugged. "They've allowed me to take on just enough fuel to reach Okinawa. Not enough for the round trip."

With fierce determination the young Ensign said, "I'm coming along, Father."

The Captain put a hand on the boy's shoulder. "Of course you feel that way, Miro. But it's not to be. I'm detaching you as of now. You are on ten-day leave which you will spend with your mother."

"But Father... Captain... Please, sir, let me come along."

"Sorry, Son." The young man embraced his father, desperately.

The father continued, "With Ken in kamikaze training and Niki in the Army you may be all your mother's got."

Miro got control of himself, and tried very hard to be a naval officer. "Yes, sir," he said in a wavering voice. "I'll take care of her, sir. You can depend on it, sir."

"Good for you, Miro."

The Captain opened the door, handed him the letter, and formally shook hands. "Take care of yourself, Son."

"You too." Miro managed to say, before stumbling blindly down the ladder.

The thump of the fuel barge pumps stopped and the huge hose—a glistening python in the rain—was retracted.

The bustle of departure seemed to occupy every one of the huge crew. Watching from the elevated position of the bridge, Captain Osaka wanted to send them all ashore. Why should good men be sacrificed because some admiral in Tokyo needed a lure for his trap?

At last a bosun's whistle blew, lines were cast off, a naval tug stood by, her engines rumbling. The air was thick with mist and the strong smell of oil. Slowly, the sharp bow swung away from the dock.

"All ahead one third," the Captain called from the out-wing of the bridge.

"All ahead one third, sir," echoed the voice of the quartermaster.

On the pier the greasy dock workers were saluting. As he passed the oil barge the Captain looked down and saw to his surprise that the barge crew was also lined up, saluting. The world seemed to know *Amato* was not returning. Osaka forced himself to concentrate on maneuvering the giant ship down the narrow channel. The presence of the huge ship in the channel was overwhelming. She seemed to command the narrow seagoing world. Her guns were mighty tapered tubes that could throw a steel projectile twenty miles. Her towering bridge rose out of sight in the lowering mist. Small sampans scurried out of her path and rocked in her wake. She carried with her a symphony of small noises. Distant bells, wireless chatter, music from focastle radios, deep throb of engines. A huge, lost community afloat. When her bow began to lift and fall, he knew she was clear. He set a course due north for Okinawa. With her rode the light cruiser Yahogi and four destroyers. Soon the night was filled with driving rain and blowing spray. Captain Osaka continued to stand outside staring into the darkness.

Miro watched his father's ship move toward the sea. Standing in the mist beside a warehouse, he could hear the deep throbbing of the engines, with an occasional small bell ringing and a piercing bosun's whistle. He hoped to see his father on the bridge, but the Captain was standing on the wrong side. He wanted to salute, but didn't do so, giving way to tears that were surging up from his heart.

After the mighty throbbing presence of *Amato* had passed and he was alone beside the warehouse, Miro felt a shiver go down his spine. Abruptly he turned and began to jog toward the city, where his orders would provide him air transportation to Tokyo.

Captain Osaka found himself calm and reflective as his ship plunged through the breathing sea. Okinawa was a full 24-hour run; she'd be there on time. She was always there when they needed her, this grey living monster now reduced to the role of a tethered goat to draw enemy tigers from the air.

Midnight. Osaka listened to the bell. Checked his wrist watch as the duty officer's voice crackled over the public address system. Four more hours until daylight. Dog watch. An assignment for ensigns, not captains. Dimly he noted the change of watch inside the bridge.

Dawn. From the east the sun now climbed through the mist. The Captain was in his cabin having taken a shower and shaved. He put on his dress white summer uniform with decorations and returned to the bridge. The young ensign saluted smartly. The Captain handed tea to the ensign, and then took a fresh cup out to the wing of the bridge. The breeze was strong; the smoke flowing straight back. By now the dark green mountains of Okinawa were visible on the horizon. He gave the order to reduce speed. The air was familiar with land smells—flowers, cooking. Osaka savored them all, inhaling deeply, listening to the ship's bells ring, engines thumping, voices crackling and the whine of the big guns trained on the landing area. He took a deep breath. Ready.

# Fourteen

Sometime after midnight I was awakened by Captain Stowell shaking my shoulder. He apologized. "Sorry, old man. The Admiral has some news." I grunted and yanked on my pants, and stumbled after him, rubbing the sleep out of my eyes. I found the Admiral grinning like a kid who's just found a quarter. He was holding a scrap of paper, which he passed on to me. "Interception of enemy transmission places battleship Amato at Okinawa in 29 hours." I read it twice and handed it back. "Now we've got a target, gentlemen," the old man said. "This time we'll sink her."

Plunging northwest towards Okinawa at twenty-five knots, *Sussex* left a skein of oily smoke between the stars and the sea. Gradually, the minute particles drifted into the water, mingling with the phosphorescence stirred by the passage of the great hull. Surface feeding fish, detecting the intrusion, cleared the course and returned to enjoy a pre-dawn toss of garbage. Aboard the ship, long before the sun would rise off her port quarter, the first activity of the day began in the galley. From there bubbling pots of coffee sent messages of hope through the ventilators and down the passageways. Sleepy men, stumbling towards heads with toothbrushes, razors, and towels, smiled as the message reached them.

It was much too early for a man to be anywhere but in a woman's arms; but the coffee was perking, and with its aroma somehow came the will to shave, shower, dress and face the day. A day that could be their most exciting, and last, if they were carrying torpedoes and rockets against a Japanese battleship, or their dullest if they were deckhands chipping rust off an anchor chain.

I smelled the coffee and lay motionless for a moment, remembering mornings in Pensacola when I would get up first and put on the pot and bring two cups to bed. Maggie would be covered up with the sheet, head and all. I would hold the steaming cup close to her and blow on it until she got a good sniff. She would whip back the sheet and sit up, with her dark hair tumbling over her face. Setting down the cups, I would smooth back her hair and kiss her. No word would be exchanged until she had swallowed at least half the cup. Then she would sigh and say, in a husky voice, "Morning, Lieutenant."

Still remembering that voice years later, I could feel my throat tighten. I checked my watch. "Time to put on your boots and march," my grandfather used to say. I sat up and swung my feet to the cold steel deck. Off you go, Mike.

Thirty minutes later, Fritz entered the wardroom, confident and ready to lead his pilots into harm's way. One by one the fliers came to breakfast. For the most part, they were quiet, each having emerged from hours of privacy, of memories, of loneliness, perhaps of dread on the eve of combat. The main noise—as they ate—was the clink of cutlery, the pouring of coffee, the squeak of the swinging door leading to the pantry, and the distant thumping of engines in some remote, nether region.

Martinez arrived late. As he dashed along the passage, recalling what had happened, he probably wanted to forego breakfast, until he realized he needed the food. It could be a long time before anybody ate again. He entered the wardroom fast and took the first seat he reached. Nobody noticed him. When his breakfast came, he ate hungrily, and drank two cups of coffee.

"Better get rid of that stuff before you take off," somebody said, touching him on the shoulder as he left.

"Good luck," somebody else said. He must have felt a surge of happiness. The day was starting right. He seemed to be accepted as one of them. Sure his ribs hurt and he probably hadn't slept much, but his spirits seemed high. He looked across at Rawlings and grinned, gratefully.

Captain McCord was having breakfast in his sea cabin. Though there was always a seat reserved for him among the senior officers in the wardroom, he frequently ate alone, reading a book propped against the silver sugar bowl. For several days now, he had been rereading passages from *Moby Dick*.

This could be the day when it happened. By nightfall, his pilots could have sunk a Japanese battlewagon. Or... with the heavily armed, evasive, and deadly fighting ship that seemed to obsess the Admiral, many of his pilots could be dead. Another reason to stay remote; eat alone and avoid getting involved with them as individuals. He liked them all. They were his people. You didn't have to know each man by name, like a scoutmaster, not to feel deep concern over the probability that he was about to die. He gave up, finished his coffee and took off for the briefing.

I finished breakfast and headed up to flag plot where I found the Admiral drinking coffee with Stowell. They were reviewing the day's op-orders. *Shenandoah's* strike would be airborne shortly. *Sussex* being closer, would have another hour. Coming from the flagship the *Sussex* CAG would be in overall command. Rawlings could get the job done if anybody could. Warming both hands with his mug, Duncan said, "Wish you were going with them, Bob?"

"Not really, Admiral," the Chief of Staff replied.

"No? Since when?"

"I'm a beaver—not an eagle."

"You expect me to believe that?" He took a swallow, "How about that Navy Cross?"

"Right place at the right time, Admiral—on the water, not the air."

The old man chuckled.

Below them the flight deck began to show signs of life. Elevators were bringing up planes for the last minute spottings. Plane crews were piling into cockpits, checking gauges, lifting cowlings, shining flashlights on engines, kicking tires, moving wing flaps, looking into magazines, tugging at bomb fastenings and torpedo releases.

The Admiral was about to attend the briefing when he changed his mind and sent me. "I did it yesterday and they came up empty. Maybe they'll think I'm bad luck."

"Let's leave it up to Fritz."

I arrived as Rawlings was finishing up his remarks. "That's it, men. We don't know about their air cover. They may be headed that way to have land-based Zeroes over them. With or without cover, they're rough. Best to deal with them like porcupines make love—very carefully." The pilots nodded at the familiar joke, and were about to break up when McCord came in. They stood; he waved them down. "I just wanted to say," his crisp, cool manner hiding his emotions—"I'm expecting every single one of you gentlemen back aboard this ship for dinner. Anyone who disobeys this order—for whatever reason—will have me to deal with."

They got the message and rewarded him with a laugh. His remarks further accentuated that this one was such a ball-buster that even the Captain was worried. In his way he had said "Good luck, fellas. Don't get yourselves killed." While they were thinking it over, McCord abruptly turned on his heel and left.

As the last of the squadron roared into the air, the Captain summoned me to the wing of the bridge and asked a question: "Have you noticed the Admiral's shortness of breath?"

"Yes, sir. Coming up the ladder. Walking on deck."

"It worries me."

"I thought it just his age."

"It's more than that. Something's wrong."

"What can be done about it?"

"I'm going to ask him to see Doc Swartz."

"Good luck."

"I'll need it."

In possible support of the Captain, despite my lowly rank, I went down to flag bridge and busied myself with charts, unit deployments and the like. The Admiral was preoccupied, studying the charts through the usual cigarette smoke screen. When McCord came, he and the Captain moved away from the OOD and other flag people—but within the hearing of the ACI officer whose concern for the Admiral's health—he hoped—forgave the misdemeanor of eavesdropping. The Captain had a direct, no-nonsense way of addressing problems. "Admiral, I'm worried about you."

"Me? The hell are you talking about?"

"Shortness of breath."

"It's this fucking carrier, Jim... Up and down. Up and down."

"I wish you'd see Dr. Swartz."

"For what? Old men wheeze and puff. I don't need a doctor to tell me the facts of life."

"I think it's more than that."

"Since when are you an M.D?"

"Swartz might have something to make you more comfortable. You're carrying a heavy burden."

"Comes with the job, McCord. The Navy trains you, brings you along. When the right billet comes, you're ready—you handle it. I've waited forty years for this post. So allow me to be a little short of breath."

"I'm not suggesting anything drastic, sir."

"*You're not.* But what about Swartz? 'Unfit for duty'—would be a bitter pill."

McCord had guts. "*Are* you unfit for duty, sir?"

"What the hell kind of question is that? Are you implying something? If so, spit it out and let's stop these fucking little innuendoes."

Calmly the Captain said, "The Admiral misunderstood the question. I was speaking of the Admiral's health. Nothing else."

"'Unfit for duty' is a goddamn dangerous fucking phrase. It's—it's a hand grenade with the pin pulled."

"Not intended that way, sir."

"Listen to me, McCord. I'm running this task force and no fucking medic is going to send me home because I'm taking in a few extra breaths!"

The Captain replied so quietly I could barely hear him.

"I'm sure that's also the last thing Dr. Swartz would want. Will you let him look at you and very possibly make you more comfortable?"

There was a long pause before the old man, sounding tired, said, "Okay, Jim. As long as he understands 'No monkey business.'"

"He'll understand, sir."

"He'd better."

David Swartz, ship's surgeon, was one of my shipboard friends, and a fellow insomniac. He had fairly decent quarters compared to mine, and, like the Captain, could usually beat me at chess, though he preferred to talk instead of juggling gambits. A rather large man with thick eyebrows, heavy glasses and a receding hairline, he had strong views. "Roosevelt's great." "Freud's a fraud." "Shakespeare's anti-Semitic."

He knew my story. "Shouldn't be here. Shouldn't be anywhere near a warship. Get yourself a dog and a cane."

I chuckled. Moved a knight. He countered instantly.

"How the hell you got a commission *plus* a sweet assignment I'll never know."

"Roosevelt's illegitimate son," I said, trying to threaten his queen.

He shook his head. "Something fishy when a guy like you ends up working for a man like Duncan."

"He's my uncle." I held my breath, hoping he'd tell me what I was yearning to hear about the old man.

"Yeah, yeah." He moved a bishop and I realized I wasn't going to hear yet. He was feeling good about something else. "Beautiful appendectomy today. One of your baby boy fliers. When I opened him up the member was about to explode in my face. I snipped it out, like clipping a red rose."

"How's the patient?"

"Doing fine. Healthy as a horse. We can hardly keep him out of a plane."

"He's lucky to have you."

"Nothing to it."

His quarters were well forward. So we got a good amount of vertical action as the bow ploughed through heavy seas. And, as in most places aboard the great ship, there was groaning, a creaking that recalled sailing ship days.

"I'm sick of this fucking war," he said after a pause. "I'm ready to get back to New York and start doing real surgery."

"Today's appendix was not 'real?'"

"It was magnificent. A work of art. No one can do it any better. But ten thousand guys could have done it—including that fellow in the sub who took out an appendix while the Captain read instructions from a fucking book.

"What I'm saying: I love these kids but I'm tired of sprained wrists and sinus infections, and broken arms. I want a brain tumor that nobody can touch but me and two other doctors in Europe. I want a heart valve that nobody has the guts to open. I want to save lives, not clear up head colds."

"Too bad you weren't in Jacksonville when I cracked up my plane."

"It's a cinch I'd have tossed you out of the Navy—that's for sure.

"My wife would have kissed you."

"I wish to hell somebody's wife would kiss me. I'm getting ready for a romp, believe me. And right now I don't care whose wife I make the move against."

"Spoken like a bachelor, David."

"Divorced. But friendly. She's also a doctor. So much for 'having things in common.'"

I chuckled. He waited a minute or two, made a queen's move, then said, at last: "Our Admiral smokes too much. He hasn't got the greatest ticker in the world, but he's so close to victory I'd hate to sideline him now."

This could be bad news. "Are you actually saying he has a bad heart?"

"He's got a fibrillating problem that I'm going to work on. Anybody else, I'd send them home. One peep outa me and he'd send me home."

"True." The old man was determined to see it through, come hell or high water.

The doctor smiled, evidently thinking of his session with the Admiral. "He's quite a guy. Up tight and ready to fight. Took a while to unwind. I finally got him laughing and the blood pressure came down. This fibrillation thing doesn't have to be a big deal—if we can hold it down. Digitalis should help. 'Gimme the straight dope,' the old man said. 'This sucker gonna kill me?'"

"'No, sir,' I said. 'We can control it. Take the pills and cut down on cigarettes.'

"'I'm too fucking busy to cut down,' he said. 'Remind me again when the war's over. I will try the pills. Thanks.'"

The doctor chuckled. One reason was his memory of the old man. The other was more obvious. "Checkmate!"

# Fifteen

In the wake of the flight the crew of the *Sussex* relaxed from the tension of the launch. Some went back to bed. Some ate ice cream. Some sought the flight deck for air. I was among these; so were Ben Nevitt and his best friend, Joe Panetta, who knew everything. He knew what the weather was going to be and why it didn't turn out as he predicted. He knew why the flight had been called back. He knew the Admiral didn't like MacArthur. He had the word. When he imparted such knowledge it was in confidence. He would look both ways as if to spot an eavesdropper, then lean in close and funnel his words into his listener's ear behind a curved hand.

"You gotta give Martinez credit," Joe said in a hoarse whisper. "Puts the fucking 'cat into the fucking ocean, damn near drowns, gets a bent rib from the dummies on the can, and today—would you believe, he's flying with the strike. Talk about balls."

Ben grinned. I had the feeling that all pilots were heroes to him. Joe again checked for eavesdroppers, although the nearest man was 30 feet away, then said, in greatest confidence, "You know what this little guy does last night at dinner? Somebody makes a crack about him ditching and Martinez tells 'em all to go fuck themselves. And him only a fucking enzyme."

Ben laughed aloud. The notion of officers cursing one another amused him. Like Joe, nobody knew so much about what went on. He decided to share his secret.

"I talked to the Admiral," Ben said, excited at the idea of telling the wonderful thing that had happened to him.

"Sure, sure," Joe said, "and I had a nice little chat with MacArthur. 'Mac,' I said, 'the trouble with you...'"

"It's true!" Ben cut in, sternly. "He sent for me to come up to the bridge and I went there. We talked about living on the farm."

Joe cocked an eyebrow. "Yeah, like me and Betty Grable gonna get married."

Ben got mad. "Mr. Mason was there. Right, sir?"

I nodded. "Right."

Joe quickly changed tactics. "You mean the fucking Admiral really sent for Ben?"

I grinned. "Why not?"

"Sonofabitch! What'd he say, Ben?"

"Nothing much. Just about the farm. And him driving a tractor too. And the war being over soon."

"Man, I like that. Getting the fuck off this tub."

"Me too. I'll be mighty glad to go home."

"You really returning to the farm?"

"Why not?"

"After being out in the world, you mean you're going back there and work your ass off raising turnips?"

"What are you going to do?" Ben asked.

"What else? Back to Little Italy, baby. That's God's country, where they drink vino rosso and watch the Yankees win the pennant."

"Who are the Yankees?"

I couldn't help laughing.

"You gotta be pulling my chain. Who are the *Yankees?* Who's the fucking president of the U.S.?"

"Mr. Roosevelt."

Joe wasn't sure that Nevitt wasn't kidding him, an action no respectable citizen of New York could tolerate. He looked at Ben suspiciously, decided Ben was hopelessly on the level. "What the hell goes with farmers? What do you do beside milk the fucking cows?"

Ben smiled again. "Plenty. We're busy from daybreak to sundown. Plowing, sowing, fertilizing, harvesting. Plenty of work, all the time. Right, Mr. Mason?"

"Absolutely."

"What do you do for fun?" Joe asked.

"We listen to the radio. Go in town to the movies Saturday nights."

"Oh brother," Joe said, awed by the horror of it all. Turning to me he said, "Unbelievable!"

For a moment our conversation lapsed, and the sounds of the ship took over. Big waves crashed against the bow as she slammed her way into the wind. Somebody started an engine, revved it up. A bosun's whistle cut through, high and piercing, followed by a garbled command. Panetta carefully extinguished his cigarette, checked for enemy spies, leaned close. "You heard about the Captain?"

"What about him?" Ben asked.

"The Admiral is driving him nuts," he said in a very conspiratorial tone. "Right, Mr. Mason?"

"I wouldn't know," I said, beginning to feel uncomfortable.

"How do you know?" Ben asked.

"I got buddies working both bridges. They hear what goes on up there. Believe me, the old man is a pistol."

"What do you mean?"

"I mean he don't just sit around with the fucking braid on his cap. He runs things. 'Bring back the fucking flight,' he says to the Captain. 'Rearm the fucking planes,' he says. 'Go get the Jap battleship. Turn on the lights.' I tell you, Ben, McCord is ready to blow his stack."

Loyally Ben said, "I like the Admiral. He's a nice fellow."

"I agree," I said. "Helluva nice fellow."

"They're all the same," Joe said with authority. "Take my word for it. Three years in the Navy. You and me—we're nothing. Just a couple of dummies the U.S. government sent out here to run their ships. We don't mean a fucking thing to those bastards. Believe me."

"Then why did the Admiral turn on the lights?" I asked.

"To save the fucking planes. Those suckers cost a million dollars apiece."

"I think he worries about the pilots," Ben said quietly.

I decided I'd better take off. Fighting the sea action, but with the wind at my back, I headed for the island.

The Captain wasn't having an easy time. It was his ship and the Admiral was his guest. With the Admiral *Sussex* had become the most important ship in the task force. All strategic commands were issued from our flag plot. Unfortunately for McCord all tactical commands— such as the Air Group recall and rearming—were also issued from *Sussex*.

Jim McCord, I had learned, won the *Sussex* assignment for his behavior at Midway and later in the Coral Sea fights. At Midway he flew a dive-bomber that set fire to a Jap carrier. As an air group leader in the Coral sea dog fights he was credited with a heavy cruiser. Later he was Exec on another big carrier.

Jim was a bachelor from Philadelphia where his family dated back to Constitution-signing days. At Annapolis he played hockey and graduated second in his class. Up to now he was on the right track to make admiral. Who knows what MacArthur's disapproval would cost him? Or Admiral Duncan's?

We were in his sea cabin, just off the main bridge in the island. Even there he remained perfectly groomed, sitting at his desk, as if I were there on business instead of an invited guest.

"How's the eye, Mike?"

"Okay, sir."

"No pain?"

"Nothing worth bothering about." A lie. The damaged eye throbbed constantly.

"You really shouldn't be here. You know that, don't you?"

"Yes, sir—you and my wife."

"You should listen to Maggie."

"Spoken like a true bachelor." He chuckled.

"Why not? Women rule the world. My Mother taught me that."

"If we'd listened to women—"

"If I'd listened to my Mother I'd be going to bed early, brushing my teeth, saying my prayers."

"Not a bad regimen it seems to me."

He drummed his fingers on his desk. "What are we going to do about the old man, Mike? Last night he had the lights on for thirty goddamn minutes, sending a signal to every Jap sub in fifty miles to come on over and have a shot."

I said nothing, having developed an admiration for the old man, yet mentally conceding the Captain's point. He continued.

"He saved some lives *and* he was lucky. Because a sub could have sunk us with 3,000 men aboard. He's a chance-taker that one. I'll be glad when the landings begin. Then maybe we'll swing him over to a cruiser."

He got up and carried his cup to the coffee pot, whose dark odors permeated the cabin, mixing with the ocean smell. He offered me a cup, which I refused, then poured himself one and returned to his desk, setting down the cup carefully on a small square of extra blotter. He saw me checking my wrist watch. "How much longer?"

"If *Amato* is at Okinawa—and I have to believe that last report—they should be getting close. Fritz'll have to throttle back—as you know—to one-fifty because of the torpeckers. Just about two hours."

He nodded and went to his own chart, where I joined him. He rapped it with his knuckles. "What a target!"

He let it go at that. But I could read the yearning of a fighting flier in his words. I suppose the ultimate target, as the old man said, is a battleship. Also the most dangerous. Did I join him in a desire to be there? Deep in my heart—hell no! It was too easy for me to see those defense guns pouring lead upwards in my direction. Maybe, as Maggie said, the training crash was doing me a favor and I was too dumb to know it. As if reading my mind, the Captain said, "What about you, Mike?

Sorry you're not there?"

I shook my head. Too late now to play games. "*Amato's* a tough customer."

"Do you wonder why she's at Okinawa?"

"Yes, sir. Wouldn't she be more useful further south?"

"If they knew our plans."

"Do you think that transmission the spy intercepted could have been deliberate?"

"I've wondered."

A faint whistle told me we were still headed south into the wind, as the bow slowly climbed a lifting sea.

The DO stuck his head in the door. "Message coming, sir."

"Thank you, Davis. Cross your fingers, Mike."

I followed the Captain to the bridge. Fritz's voice, fuzzy with distance: "Swimmer One calling Mother Shark. Come in Mother Shark."

McCord took the microphone. "This is Mother Shark. We read you Swimmer. Over."

Fritz again: "Engaging enemy ships at Okinawa as briefed. Force of One *Amato* Class Battleship, plus a heavy cruiser, four cans."

"Roger. Mother Shark copies. Good luck. Out."

# Sixteen

*Bull elephant falling*
*Many carnivores come*
*Thirsting for the kill*

Having written his wife, sent his son ashore, obeyed the High Command and brought his ship to be sacrificed, Captain Osaka felt strangely detached. He knew what was going to happen, yet he felt remote from it— as though he were familiar with a tragic play about to be acted but more as a member of the audience than a key player. In this mood he was able to function as Commander of the mighty war vessel almost reflexively, while pursuing a procession of thoughts totally unmilitary in nature.

For many moments, while supervising bridge activities in his usual quiet, efficient way, he recalled in great detail the building of the family schooner. He recalled hiring the services of a master shipbuilder, a very old man with a sharp eye and a gentle way of handling teak as if it were the skin of a woman. He smiled as he saw, in retrospect, the brown-limbed presence of his sons, as they scampered over the boat obeying the master builder. When, after many months the schooner was finished, he arranged a proper launching at which the old man said a prayer calling upon the forces of the sea to be kind to those who sailed in the schooner. He needed the old man's prayer today.

Captain Osaka, on the wing of the bridge, saw the divebombers and hoped his high-speed turn would cause a miss. When the bombs struck the forward deck, he instinctively flinched, struck the rail with his fist. Everywhere he looked *Amato* was defending herself. Her gunners were at their weapons, pumping shells into the attacking aircraft. Firefighters were dragging hoses, spraying water on flames. In the wheelhouse the quartermaster was doing his best to obey the officer of the day in making *Amato* an elusive target.

The Captain swung to the opposite wing of the bridge and looked aft. All hands were engaged. Dozens, probably hundreds of men swarmed over the huge deck dragging hoses, carrying the wounded, firing guns, putting up a continuous wall of anti-aircraft shellbursts, some of which exploded close overhead with a steady roar, augmented by the scream of diving enemy planes and the sharp crack of detonating bombs. Osaka had to yell at his quartermaster to guide the great vessel out of harm's way—an impossible task that each man accepted as part of the violent scene in which they were playing roles.

Everywhere the Captain looked blue enemy aircraft poured out of the sky in an endless stream. His defensive fire exacted its toll, blowing some blue planes to bits in mid-air, sending others into the sea trailing smoke and flame.

As the volume of noise reached its peak—defensive guns and their exploding shells, offensive planes and their bombs and machine guns—the Captain had to give up leadership from the bridge. Unable to be heard directly, he left it up to his officers and crew on station to keep up the defenses, gather the wounded and fight the growing fires.

He knew the torpedo bombers would strike soon. He watched three of them explode in the face of *Amato's* guns, each earning a growled "well done, lads." Finally one torpedo hit home and Osaka heard the deep engine room explosion at almost the same moment as the plane that released it was hit, drawing from Osaka a grim unspoken compliment to his gunners. He had the phone in hand to learn the damage when another torpedo burst into the engine room cutting off the chief engineer in mid-sentence.

After a brief pause, during which the Captain waited patiently, a shaky voice came on the phone. "Sir, this is Toburi. The Chief has been killed. We are taking water in two places. Twenty men are dead."

"Listen to me," the Captain shouted. "Get everybody out of there! Do you read me, Toburi? Abandon ship. Abandon ship! Acknowledge."

"Aye, sir. Abandon ship. I'll do my best, Captain."

Captain Osaka could picture the flooded engine room. He winced as he realized his friend, the Chief Engineer, was among the dead. He prayed the survivors would get out; or was it too late already? Could anything capsize such a ship? The assumption had always been no. As he felt her begin to list to starboard the full horror of the situation struck him. Those two torpedoes exploding deep below the water line had opened her to the sea and the sea was pulling her down on the right-hand side. She was going over.

From his position on the bridge he realized—in the midst of on-going defensive fire and continuingly exploding bombs, a deafening cannonade—

that the bridge tower was dipping toward the sea—an occurrence so hard to accept that he watched in awe, as if it were some kind of unspeakable three-demensional movie. In this brief spectator role he saw his crew begin to jump ship, running and diving into the water, desperate men close by, tiny figures swarming over the far reaches of the tilting deck. God! How could such a nightmare be happening?

The speed of this overturn seemed to increase as the main bridge, to which he clung, tilted closer to the water. When he was a few feet above the waves he realized that his guns had been silenced. Keep firing, boys! Keep firing!

Then the bridge went under and he automatically began to swim. All around him the crew splashed in noisy confusion, calling out friend to friend, helping one another inflate life vests, holding up the wounded.

The Captain saw the keel rising in air, seeming freshly polished, naked, almost obscene; something you don't look at—like the nether parts of a senior woman caught by the breeze.

He realized that there would be a terrible suction as she sank. Recognizing two of his officers he shouted, "Get the men away from here. Move the men away!"

They understood him and slowly began to round up the swimming crewmen who had been attempting to climb back aboard the capsized ship.

The Captain himself took part in the endeavor, finally realizing it was a hopeless task and becoming aware that the great ship had already, very slowly, begun to rotate. When she went down, she would create a terrible vortex, a spinning suction almost beyond belief--yet hard for a swimming crewman to imagine with sufficient clarity to keep him from attempting to scramble aboard.

As long as his strength held out Captain Osaka moved along the ship's edge waving his men away, enlisting his officers in the task. As the vortex increased he realized it was a lost cause. Everywhere he looked exhausted men lay face down on the exposed bottom with its two huge brass propellers looming above. Two of his senior officers came to him begging him to save himself. He firmly refused and ordered them back into the water.

With a sudden downward movement the *Amato* swept everybody into the sea and the Captain now swam beside his crewmen. He spit out a mouthful of water and shouted—pointing away from the ship—"Swim. Swim." Obediently most of his crewmen tried to escape the pull of the suction. Some succeeded. Captain Osaka did not.

# Seventeen

I was with Captain McCord when the flight began to come aboard. Among the first dozen there was a torpecker from which the pilot emerged with a bloody shoulder. I recognized Stone and hurried forward, arriving simultaneously with two medics and a stretcher. Stone, who had been inspecting the damage of his plane, looked up at the medics and said, "You can secure that stretcher. Just get me to the doc who'll take this fucking bullet outa my shoulder." They shrugged, folded up the stretcher and one took each arm. He saw me and said, "Well, you're johnny-on-the-spot. Ready for your debriefing?"

"Not really, Jesse. I saw you had been shot—"

"Not bad," he said. "We sank her; write that down. One Thirteen sank the fucking battleship."

The medics were moving him away.

"Congratulations," I said. Then somehow feeling inadequate, I called out, "Good work, Jesse."

He was disappearing through a watertight door and made no reply. I wasn't sure he heard me.

I found Martinez in the ready room. He was still pumped up, so much so he paced the room like a caged animal. "Well, sir, we took off and lined up behind Mr. Rawlings. He had told us to throttle back so we wouldn't outrun the torpeckers who can only do one-fifty. So we all formed up—the bunch from *Shenandoah* and *Winchester* too—and believe me it made you proud to see all those fucking aircraft. 'Here come the Americans,' I thought. I wanted to speed on ahead but old Fritz said no. I was glad to be with the group in spite of the ribs."

The mention of ribs took away his grin. He poured himself a cup of coffee and sat down, wincing. "Well, sir, we got to Okinawa, nice green island—and there she was, the biggest fucking battleship in the whole world. Scared the living hell out of me. No more need for radio silence so old Fritz comes on, cool and calm, with, 'Okay, boys. Remember what I told you, dive bombers first, torpeckers last.' God almighty, it was like a movie. The bombers pushed over and started down. Fritz right behind. Then me and the others. Talk about a thrill! In seconds the ack-ack was everywhere. Black puffs all over the fucking sky. Diving straight into their fucking guns. I dropped my bombs and strafed the gun crews as I crossed the deck. Saw Fritz unload, then turn his fifties on the bridge. Terry was right behind. God almighty we really raised hell with those exposed gunners. Then I was climbing outa there and Old Fritz didn't want us to repeat because we had to cover for the bombers and torpeckers. Once I was on top again I saw a terrible thing happen—I saw Lamont's plane explode. Made me sick. One minute Duke was yelling that his torpedo had hit the ship. Next minute he was a ball of fire. My God, it was awful, Mr. Mason." He choked up and his eyes filled with tears.

A divebomber took up the report. "We went down first. Blew the bridge apart, knocked a hole in the forward deck big enough to drop in a freight car. I damn near blew myself up not pulling out soon enough. I can still hear Fritz yelling, 'Pull up, you crazy bastard.'"

It was at least an hour before Fritz was available. Our debriefing took place in his room where his adrenalin was also still pumping. He began with Lamont the torpedo pilot whose plane exploded. "You never saw anything like it. The kid—had just stuck a fish into the ship and was yelling his head off when—pow—his torpecker explodes. Goddamndest thing. He's gone. Like that." Fritz pulled off his wet shirt and threw it across the room. "What do I say to his mother?"

He sat on the bed. "You never saw such a fucking bunch of guns. Like a porcupine. Boom! Boom! Boom! Couldn't see the fucking ship for the smoke. I said to myself, 'She's gonna kill us all. This is suicide.' I don't know how many guys they got. My count is ten so far. Probably more. Plus Vernon."

"They got Terry?" I said, feeling a sudden sense of loss.

"He's down, but I made a pass over him and at least he's in his raft."

"Good."

Fritz went on "he and I followed the dive bombers down and then stayed upstairs looking for enemy fighters.

"When they arrived, we mixed it up with 'em at first and then realized they were amateurs. Terry must have shot down at least three of 'em when a bullet from somewhere set his fighter on fire. I followed him down and saw him bail out and hit the water. When I last saw him he was crawling into the raft."

"Can we get a PBY in there?" I asked.

"Sure gonna try!"

I waited to hear what happened to *Amato*. In a changed tone Fritz continued. "Lamont's fish blew a hole in the port side, but Stone killed her."

"Stone?" Why should I be surprised?

He nodded, "Yep. That cocky little bastard came down low, ducked around a waterspout and fired his fish. I could see the trail of bubbles going straight. Held my breath as he overflew the shot and jumped across her deck. Man, I want to tell you when that fucking torpedo hit that ship all living hell broke loose. Must have reached a powder magazine because the goddamn battleship just seemed to come apart. Nobody who saw it will ever forget. She turned over. I mean capsized with the fucking keel in the air and guys scrambling to climb. Dozens of 'em. Hundreds. Christ what a mess. Then Stone gets shot. Here's what happened. He climbs up near where I was just as a bunch of Zeroes jump us and one of 'em puts a round through his canopy from above. I knew he was hit but couldn't tell how bad. Glad he made it home okay.

"Come back in an hour. I'd like a shave and we'll talk about awards."

"Okay."

"First, do me a favor?"

"Sure."

"Take these coordinates to the Captain. That's about where Terry went in. See if we can have a catalina pick him up."

"Right."

The Captain listened to my story, then went to his wall chart and quickly found the spot.

"Pretty long run, Mike."

"Yes, sir."

"But not responsible."

"No, sir."

"Terry's a good man. Let's see what our land-based friends think. Tell Fritz we'll try."

"Thank you, sir."

I returned to find Fritz working on a list in his cabin dressed only in boxer shorts. He was pacing up and down with a wad of paper in one hand and a pen in the other. The room smelled of aftershave, a spicy change from the oil and gasoline odors of the passage. He stopped in front of me and shook the wad of paper. "Stone," he said.

"What about him?"

"Like I told you, he sank the fucking ship and turned her over."

"So what's the problem?"

"So? He deserves a Navy Cross. But he's such a shit, and now he's also a fucking wounded hero."

"He sank the ship. Give him a medal."

"He'll get it. Don't worry." He snorted. "We lost Lamont and Stone comes out smelling like a rose. Talk about justice."

"And Duke?"

"I'm recommending a posthumous Navy Cross."

"Okay. Shall I do the letter for you?"

"I'll do it. The mother is quite a lady. I met her back in Pearl."

"Finished the list?"

He handed it to me and I glanced down. Martinez was getting a DFC. So were a long list of others, some who already had DFCs were getting gold stars.

I grinned. "He's a good kid."

"Marty? He did all right."

"Glad you gave him a second shot."

"You never know. This time it worked out. Everybody did great."

In his sea cabin over a cup of coffee the Captain looked at the awards list. "This Stone fellow. He the one who came up here and made a fool of himself?"

"Yes, sir. But it looks like he's better at handling a torpedo."

The smell of fresh coffee filled the room. "Crusty little bastard, isn't he?"

"Yes, sir. He says it like it is."

"Too bad his mother didn't teach him better manners."

"I guess she did the best she could—up there in the coal fields."

"Hard life I suppose." We could hear a bosun's whistle and a distant engine revving up. "Is he married?"

"No, sir. At least not that anybody knows of. He gets no mail."

"Lonely little bugger—with a chip on his shoulder. That it?"

"That's it, sir."

"Fritz credits him with the *coup de grace* for the *Amato*."

"Right." He shook his head and thumped down his cup. "I hate to see our highest award go to a fellow like that."

"Point is, sir, he earned it, warts and all."

"I know. I know."

I hesitated, then said, "The Navy Cross isn't exactly a club, is it Captain?"

"In a way. Yes, goddamnit. It's a club with the toughest possible entry fee—you have to perform an act of bravery in combat—over and beyond the call of duty."

"I mean it must include all kinds of men—not just 'officers and gentlemen.'"

"Don't be ridiculous. I know that. Good Christ, look at the Marines that have won it. Kids right out of a barnyard with stout hearts and no nerves."

"Fritz wants him to have it—even though there's no love lost between them."

The Captain returned the list. "Tell him to take it to the Admiral. You say Stone is ambulatory? Can he make it to the flight deck?"

"I'll find out, sir."

I returned to Fritz's cabin as he was shrugging into a fresh shirt. "Let's go break the news to Jesse," he said, buttoning the shirt.

We found Stone sitting on his bed in the infirmary with a large bandage over his left shoulder and another halfway down his chest under the left arm. He was writing a letter and when we entered, he frowned, put down his pen and looked at each of us as if we'd come to arrest him.

"How's it going?" Fritz said.

Stone didn't quite manage a shrug owing to his bandages. "Okay," he said.

Fritz cleared his throat. "Got some news for you, Jesse."

Stone waited.

"I'm recommending you for a Navy Cross."

Stone looked at Fritz, looked at me, and ran a hand over his face.

Fritz went on. "You fired the torpedo that did the damage. You earned it."

Stone picked up the letter he was writing. "Lamont's mother"—he began. "I was just—"

He came to a dead stop. Then in a husky voice he said, "You recommended me for the *Navy Cross?* That's what you said?"

"That's what I said."

"Jesus." He scratched the back of his head. After a long pause filled with carrier sounds, the most predominant of which was distant hangar deck screeching, he said, "What about Duke? He hit the ship too."

Fritz said, "I'm also recommending one for him."

Stone picked up his letter. I wondered if Fritz was thinking what I was thinking. We'd both ignored the fact that Stone was Lamont's squadron leader and he was the one to send the letter—not Fritz.

"Congratulations, Jesse," I said.

"Thanks," he said, almost in a whisper.

In a business-like tone Fritz said, "The ceremony is tomorrow. Think you can make the flight deck?"

Stone said, "I'll be there."

"Take care of that shoulder," Fritz said.

"Sure," Stone said in a small voice. "I'll be there, Commander."

Our visit to Martinez was different—to say the least. We found him lying on his bunk. The rosary was back on the crucifix and the tiny room barely admitted the bulk of two visitors. Marty leaped from his bunk, snatched a pair of tan trousers from the only chair, and yanked them on. "Gentlemen, come in. *Por favor,* please come in." He smoothed up the bed as Fritz took the chair and I stood by the dresser.

Sounding much more natural, Fritz said, cheerfully, "Got some news for you, Marty."

"Sir?"

"You did well out there, attacking the ship and shooting down the Zeroes afterwards."

"Thank you for taking me along."

Fritz grinned, "I'm recommending you for DFC."

Marty's eyebrows came together, "DFC?"

Fritz laughed. "That's Distinguished Flying Cross, you ignorant Mexican bastard."

Marty said, smiling, "Ignorant *American* bastard."

"Congratulations, Marty," I said—speaking the only line I seemed to be capable of. It was after all, Fritz's moment. Christmas, with the CAG as Santa.

"Thanks, Mr. Mason."

"Flight deck at zero-nine-hundred," Fritz said.

"Right, sir. *Muchas Gracias.* Thank you, sir."

For the next hour we visited the many other men who had won DFCs. Then the familiar call came on the P.A. system. "Lieutenant Mason to flag bridge. Lieutenant Mason to flag bridge."

I arrived, as usual, out of breath from the climb and from stepping through so many watertight doors. The Admiral wasn't happy. He looked up from a dispatch. "They tricked us, Mason. That intercept from the spy pinpointing Okinawa?"

"Yes, sir?"

"They sent *Amato* there on purpose to pull away planes so they could hit our carriers. Look at this. They set fire to *Shenandoah,* set fire to *Belmont,* sank *Princeton,* sank *Dover Bay.* Sank *Hilton Head.* Goddamnit to hell!"

I took the dispatch and read it in disbelief. They'd tricked us; at what price? Incredible! The Admiral took back the dispatch and shook it angrily. "Used their goddamn biggest battleship like an antelope tied to a stake to get a tiger. And we obliged."

There wasn't much I could say or do. I waited for the wind to change.

When the old man slapped down the dispatch and the Chief of Staff picked it up, I decided to bring up a new subject. "Awards list, sir."

The old man took it from me and put on the glasses. "The top name on their list," he said, "should be the captain of *Amato*, I salute him."

He began to read the names, half aloud, nodding approval. When he finished he looked at me, raising his brows. I said, "If the Admiral approves, tomorrow at zero-nine-hundred on the flight deck?"

"Very well. Pass the word."

The ceremony went along briskly, starting promptly at zero-nine-hundred. The Captain didn't want to take the crew off their jobs and turn it into a full dress affair; we were, after all, in a war zone. So a small area was marked off and a crowd of recipients assembled there, in fresh tan uniforms. Among them Martinez and moving slowly, Jesse Stone, with his jacket draped over his shoulders and his bandage showing underneath.

The Admiral and Captain stood at the base of the island, with the wind pushing at their uniforms. The Captain, with jacket, seemed the perfect model of a naval officer; the Admiral, still in zippered blue rain jacket and wearing the baseball cap, was himself. Fritz, with uniformed coat, lined up his fliers, spun on his heel like a true Annapolis man, marched over to the two senior officers and saluted. "The awards recipients of Air Group One Thirteen are present and accounted for, gentlemen."

The Captain: "Very well, Commander." Turning to the Admiral, he said, "Shall we proceed, sir?"

The Admiral said, "Proceed," and turned to his Chief of Staff who was holding the medals in an open box. Fritz led the Admiral and Captain Stowell to the line of fliers standing unnaturally at attention. As the Admiral approached he grinned, and called out, "At ease, gentlemen. Just relax. I want to thank you for what you did and tell you the Navy is proud of you."

Slowly the old man went along the column, reading the wording of the award, taking the medal from his aide, pinning it on the flier, shaking hands, returning the salutes of the smiling young men. When he reached Stone, he accepted the award from Stowell, read it aloud and carefully pinned it to Stone's jacket, which was draped across his shoulders. He then shook hands and said something I couldn't hear. Two more wounded men were in the line. The Admiral treated each of them the same way. Martinez was last. His smile was wide enough to land an F6F in. I could see the Admiral's response, a twinkle in his eye as he came back to stand beside the Captain. Fritz, back in the Annapolis role, called out, "Attention," spun on his heels and marched over to the other officers. "Permission to dismiss the company, sir?"

The Admiral said, "One moment, Commander." He reached inside the box and drew out an award with a blue and white ribbon.

While Fritz stood frozen at attention the Admiral walked over and pinned on the Navy Cross. The fliers cheered spontaneously. The Captain came forward and joined the Admiral patting Fritz on the back and shaking hands. When they were finished the fliers broke ranks and clustered around Fritz. Among them, I was happy to notice, was a short man with a bandage on his left shoulder. When he had finished, as he turned to make his way back to his infirmary, Captain McCord went over and stuck out his hand. "Congratulations, Lieutenant Stone."

"Thank you, sir." Jesse was smiling.

The Captain didn't forget his invitation to the Air Group. They were to be his guests for dinner. It was a happy occasion, made the more so at the start by a shot of brandy for every pilot—as prescribed by the medical officer after a hard and hazardous flight. Standard procedure for battle zone doctors and the young fliers.

Somehow, the supply of brandy didn't seem to dry up after the medicinal shots; the Captain failed to notice it—despite the pitch of the laughter among the pilots and the frequency of little speeches from the youngsters who'd get to their feet, raise a water glass, and say, "Here's to the *Sussex*" or "Here's to Bomber One Thirteen" or "Torpedo One Thirteen". Finally Fritz stood up and proposed a toast "to the Captain"—which brought the party to its feet with shouts of "Captain".

The Captain's response was a simple "I'm proud to have you aboard."

Just before the party was over Jesse Stone rose to his feet. He still had his coat over his shoulders and his bandages were visible. A sudden quiet fell over the pilots, as if they sensed something was about to happen. He raised a water glass as the others had done, then took a drink and thumped it down, spilling a little. "Captain McCord, Commander Rawlings and gentlemen of One Thirteen," he began quietly, raising the glass again, "Let's drink to the men who didn't make it. Duke Lamont, Ted Wilson, Buck Newton..." He recited all the names almost angrily, as if they'd done something wrong.

When he finished the Captain stood and held up his waterglass. "Here, here."

Everybody stood up with raised glasses and repeated, "Here, here."

Jesse stood looking into the distance and then left the wardroom, moving slowly, as his wound dictated.

I had a sudden impulse to follow Jesse back to his room in the infirmary.

"There you are!" the corpsman greeted him. "You're supposed to be in bed.".

"That's where I'm going."

"I mean you shouldna' left. The doctor was furious."

"Fuck him," Jesse said.

I felt sorry for the corpsman, who seemed very young and vulnerable as he stalked out of the room.

"You were rough on him, Jesse," I said.

"I guess so," Jesse said. "Kid worries too much."

In the brief pause that followed we could feel the bow quite close, climbing a big wave, making the ship creak like a schooner. The smell was—for once—not gasoline but carbolic acid, I assumed. That hospital odor that says to a germ, "You're a goner!"

"What do you want, Lieutenant?" Jesse asked abruptly.

"Nothing special," I said, somewhat put off by his directness. "Just wanted to be sure you got back here okay."

"You think I needed a wet nurse?"

"Forget it, Jesse. No big deal."

"I can't figure you out, Mason. One minute you wanna fight. Next you come sucking around."

I was on my feet. "Fuck you, Stone. A guy tries to be your friend..."

"Relax, relax. Don't be so touchy."

I took the jacket that had been hanging from his shoulders and hung it in the closet. He began unbuttoning his shirt. I figured I'd better not try to help with that. He looked up with a sudden grin. "How about that fucking Navy Cross?"

"Nice going," I said.

"You shoulda seen that ship," he said. "Biggest fucking thing you ever laid eyes on. I'm surprised a fucking torpedo could knock her over."

I let him relive the moment, then asked the question I'd been wanting to ask. "You still think you'll be getting out?"

He had the shirt off now and I took it from him. He wagged his close-cropped head. "Goddamn if I know. There's nothing on the outside like flying a fucking torpecker. Maybe a motorcycle, but you don't get paid to do that. We'll have to see when the war is over."

Wearing only his shorts and wincing with pain, he eased into the bed.

"I'm glad you made that toast," I said.

"Felt like a jackass. Then I said to myself, 'Here we are with a shot of brandy in our belly and a steak dinner, everybody laughing and making toasts and those guys deader than herrings down there with the fucking fish and it don't look like anybody gives a shit.'"

"Good night, Jesse."

"Yeah," he said, "Give my regards to the Admiral."

Dr. Swartz had his hands full with Lieutenant Stone. "Who does this little shit think he is?" the doctor roared, as we stood together taking the air in a gun tub. "I cut out a round, sew him up, tell him to stay in bed. First thing I know he's getting dressed and on his way to a ceremony on deck. Navy Cross, if you please. What does the blood system know from Navy Crosses? You move around, your wound comes open. You gotta be still. I tell him this, he says—you guessed it—'fuck you, Commander.' Good thing I didn't have a scalpel handy. Now who do I see drinking my brandy at the Captain's dinner? The walking hemorrhage, himself. 'Hi doc,' he says and raises his glass to me. Wait'll that thing comes apart. I'll just stand there and laugh while he bleeds to death."

"He's a cocky one." I say. "A hard nut."

"I know the type. Small dog with big bark."

"And big bite. Ask the Captain of the *Amato*."

"Sure, sure. Brave as hell but scared to death somebody'll get behind their protective armor."

"In Stone's case that would take a bit of doing. You'd need a hammer and chisel."

"Or a pretty woman."

"Right." A pause, during which we both breathed deep the sweet salt air.

"How are the wounded?"

"Not bad. You know, of course, we lost eleven but the ones that managed to get back—carrying Jap lead—have all been taken care of. One rather tricky placement. I took a bullet out of the kid's spine. Another fraction of a fraction and he'd have been paralyzed."

"Better than curing colds?"

He smiled. "Much better."

# Eighteen

We were at lunch when the Captain tapped on a glass and the chatter stopped. The Captain began mock-seriously, "You will recall, gentlemen, that I invited you to dinner and promised to deal with those who failed to attend. I've just had word that one absentee will make it after all." He paused and smiled, "Terry Vernon has been picked up."

A tremendous roar erupted. I joined in, fighting back tears. God bless those big ugly PBYs!

Terry didn't reach the carrier until late afternoon. I watched him high wire from the destroyer after being flown to a temporary naval base in Pindoro Point. When word spread that he was coming across, the entire air group was there to greet him. Rawlings and I embraced him with a bear hugs and the others banged him on the arm, shook his hand, patted his shoulder. When the greetings were over, Fritz said, "Captain wants to see you."

I tagged along out of sheer curiosity. As we arrived the Captain came over to him with an extended hand.

"Welcome back, Terry."

"Thank you, sir. Glad to be here."

The Captain smiled and took a folded paper from his pocket. "Message for you."

Terry unfolded and read the message, then looked up and grinned. "It's a girl. How about that? I got me a baby girl."

I smiled. The officer of the deck smiled. The quartermaster at the wheel smiled. The Captain smiled. It was a proud moment.

"One more thing," the Captain said, reaching in his pocket and taking out a DFC.

"You missed the ceremony. Congratulations."

A pleasant sight. The small Captain in his immaculate uniform, pinning the red white and blue medal on the huge chest of Terry Vernon still in the wrinkled clothes of his dunking.

After he'd had a few hours sleep Terry and I met in the ward room for debriefing.

As Terry told it, with frequent chuckles: "These life rafts are for average-size guys, not types like me. I watched the formation disappear and wanted to yell, 'Hey, fellas, wait for me.' I was hot, wet and sticky. I took a drink from the canteen. Tepid. Half full. Better take it easy. Found a compass. Fishing stuff. Two aluminum paddles. Took one. Headed north where the clouds were. Land.

"Thunderstorm hit me. Fresh water but lost ground from the wind. Blew me back toward east. Rain felt good. Cool. Thought about Tony. The baby.

"Suddenly a Japanese swimmer, for God's sake, half drowned. Tried to help him. He bit me! Fuck him. Let him drown. Can't do that. Bastard unconscious. Up close no movement. Decided to tie him to raft. Fishing line. Just a kid. Came to. Gave him a drink. Fucking raft too small for me. No room for two. Why screw up my chances? Rigged a sail with shirt. Dragged him along like a big fish I'd caught.

"Jap plane buzzed us. Guy woke up, yelled. Plane returned and came low. Flew off. Trouble?

"He struggled to break fishing line. Then we both heard another plane. Turned out to be a good old Navy PBY. I yelled and they came in to land. The Jap struggled like crazy, broke the fishing line. Dove out of sight.

"The Catalina took me aboard. Pilot said, 'What about raft?'

"I said, 'Leave it'.

"As we took off I saw the Jap swimming towards the raft."

# Part II

# Nineteen

*March, 1945*

> *Peony petal*
> *Falls into clear garden pool*
> *Wet ant finds life raft*

In a spacious house overlooking the sea the Captain's wife Kei listened to the caller on the phone. The grocer's wife was calling—with profuse apologies for disturbing Mrs. Osaka. When the amenities were over, the grocer's wife came to the point: her son was home.

"How lovely!" Mrs. Osaka said.

"Not so lovely," the grocer's wife said. "He has been injured. In fact," her voice broke, "he is paralyzed."

"I am so very sorry," Mrs. Osaka said. "How can I help?"

"He wants to see you. He has a message from your son."

"From Niki? A message from Niki?"

"Could you come to us? Please?"

"Of course. Right away. I'll come at once."

In western dress—skirt, blouse and yellow raincoat—Mrs. Osaka, under a pale green paper umbrella, made her way into town. She found the grocer's house near his shop and there, in an immaculate room, lay a pale youth propped up by saffron pillows. His mother, wearing a clean thread-bare kimono, bowed her welcome. Covered by a white sheet, the son smiled and said huskily, "Thank you for coming, Mrs. Osaka. I cannot rise to greet you."

The house smelled of fish soup. Mrs. Osaka sat by the bed and touched his shoulder.

"You are a friend of Niki?"

"Yes, ma'am. We were together in the Army pilot training school. I crashed a plane." He gestured to his leg lying motionless under the sheet. "I was never very good. They were always shouting at us."

"How is Niki?" Mrs. Osaka asked, uncomfortable that the mother remained standing as if she were a servant awaiting orders.

"Niki is fine," the grocer's son said, smiling. "He flies like a bird. Everybody says he's the best."

"Can you tell me what's going on?"

"Yes, ma'am," he said bitterly. "The Army was training us to die for our country. We were all supposed to volunteer like the Navy, but it didn't work that way. Our commander just called us together and told us we were volunteers. He said we didn't have to do it, but the fellows who tried to get out were beaten. Niki was beaten."

Mrs. Osaka felt her heart turn over. Poor Niki. First her husband, then Kenishi—were they still alive? "The message?" The boy lowered his voice. "Niki said to tell you he was *not* going to be a kamikaze."

She raised her eyebrows, "What did he mean?"

"I'm not really sure, ma'am, but I'll tell you what we used to whisper about at night when everybody else was asleep."

Mrs. Osaka waited.

"The Philippines are nothing but islands, hundreds of islands. We figured we'd just get lost in the clouds one day and find an island. He's good at navigation. We'd make it back. I was sure of that until this happened."

Mrs. Osaka remembered Niki's skill with the family sailboat. Dare she allow herself to hope? She leaned over and kissed the youngster on the cheek.

"Thank you."

"He meant it, ma'am. He can do it."

"I'm sure he can," Mrs. Osaka said quietly. As she left the rain had stopped and the sun was out. She snapped her umbrella shut and began to walk briskly.

Striding home through the crowded streets she recalled the summer Niki and two other 10-year-olds had set out to walk a hundred miles. It was June and Niki had persuaded his best friends at school that this was a challenge not to be avoided. Two other parents had to be persuaded—all of which was duly accomplished—and one warm morning the three of them stood beside the Osaka family car to have their pictures taken, three tiny boy-men dressed like mountain climbers with packs on their backs and walking sticks. When all three families had their share of snapshots, she had driven the boys to the tiny village of Tendira, exactly one hundred miles from Tokyo. They climbed out of the car, running loose like puppies for a moment then seriously bowing and shaking hands. As she got back in the car and looked at them, waving and saluting, she wondered how she'd been persuaded to do this. But, sure enough, five days later—Niki having predicted twenty miles a day—there they were, a bit bedraggled and somehow an inch taller, three dead tired little boys full of pride and blisters, but proud, happy, and starved.

# Twenty

An air of excitement ran through the ship as *Sussex*, holding off Okinawa, turned into the wind for predawn take-offs. Few of the pilots had gotten any sleep. As usual, I had briefed them. Their first job was to hit enemy gun emplacements; then the fighters were to furnish cover for the troop landings. At this point Japanese air capability was a mystery. Intelligence reports indicated that she had lost most of her experienced fliers, but with Japan you never knew.

Admiral Duncan was like a racehorse on Derby Day. He left his quarters long before take-off time, probably wishing he could be in one of the planes. With a cup of coffee in hand he stepped onto the flag bridge, feeling the cool lingering night wind, smelling the land, rotting vegetation, wood smoke. On the deck below, the huge strike force was in position, wheels chocked, fuel tanks topped off, magazines loaded, waiting for their pilots. An elevator rose, klaxons wailing. As *Sussex* headed for land with the wind in her face, ship smells mingled with the incoming breeze. Gasoline and oil. Smoke from the engines below. Laundry soap. Coffee. The Admiral raised his nose like an old hound and seemed to savor it all. "Ever hear of the Gettysburg Reunion, son?"

"Yes, sir. We have a picture of my grandfather in a dark cleric's suit wearing a reunion hat."

He smiled. "My father took me. I was just a kid. We rode the train. Windows open. Summertime. Lots of cinders. I can hear the cinders crunching under the conductor's shoes." He paused remembering the cinders. "My father was a captain. Lots of his men came up and shook hands. Some saluted. He knew them all by name.

"At night, there were campfires and singing. Later, at Annapolis, I learned that more than 60,000 soldiers had fallen on those fields and I wondered why the survivors had gone back to celebrate such a terrible event. But, as a youngster, I listened to the songs and, looking at the faces in the light of the campfires, I envied them—the thrill of having been in America's greatest battle. On the way home my father finally spoke of his own role:

"'Our company was supposed to go up the hill after the shelling. You never heard such a noise. More than one hundred guns. It was like the end of the world. You couldn't hear yourself think. "Old Longstreet's giving 'em hell," somebody shouted. I didn't see how any Yankees could be still alive up there on the ridge. Because I was young and foolish I actually was sorry there wouldn't be anybody left for me to shoot at.'"

His father had paused, Duncan recalled, and then in a changed voice had said, "I needn't have worried. There were plenty of them left. We lost half our company before it was over."

The voice of the Admiral's father, reaching him across the years, still carried quiet heartbreak.

Captain Stowell appeared on the flag bridge, his pipe gleaming in the dark. "Good morning, Admiral. Morning, Mike."

The Admiral and I murmured, "Morning," and the old man said, "You ready for me?"

"Yes, sir." They went inside and leaned over a chart marked with arrows and circles in grease pencil. Stowell pointed with his pipe stem. "Fleet dispositions as you instructed, Admiral. Missouri will initiate bombardment from here." The pipe stem aimed at the big battleship's assigned spot. "She's a fat target, so here's her screen cruisers and cans—just in case their subs get nosey. Near the point, as you designated, troop transports and their screen. This clutter, of course, landing craft. Everything according to the book, sir."

"I wonder if the Japs have read the book?" the Admiral said.

Stowell said, "Let's hope not, sir."

"All right, Bob. Carriers on station?"

"Yes, sir. Our position is *here* as base for the first wave. *Tarpon Springs* and *Charleston* are west of us as marked."

"Good." The old man lit a cigarette and covered the chart with smoke, as if in prelude to battle. In his mind's eye did he see the huge armada spread across the dark sea? Waiting for the sun? Waiting to retake the island from the Japanese? I could picture the young men in the transports trying to sleep in the foul air of crowded bunkrooms. Young men who might die this day far from home, with machine gun bullets ripping through their helmets. Maybe this would be the end of the killing. How much longer can those Japanese hold out? Just the sight of this attack force alone should send them running to the Emperor begging for peace. Dream stuff; they never gave up. The Admiral returned to his bridge, searching for the first signs of daybreak.

Jim McCord also got up early. He dressed carefully, and arrived on the bridge in fresh khakis and with his shoes polished. I wondered if he had a sense of history about the day that hadn't yet dawned. He and his ship were about to be part of a giant invasion that could end the war. I could see *Sussex* sailing into San Francisco Bay with her full complement manning the rail on the flight deck in dress whites; bands would be playing and tugboats shooting water into the sky and banners hanging down from the Golden Gate Bridge.

I could even see Maggie on the dock with the girls standing on either side looking beautiful and waving proudly. We'd drive to a good hotel like the Mark Hopkins, and have a wonderful dinner; and when the girls had gone to sleep, Maggie and I would be together in the darkness and I would show her what a sailor can do when he's been away from his woman too long. Then we would lie in each other's arms listening to the sounds of the city, the street car bells, harbor fog horns, police sirens, maybe music from Chinatown.

On the bridge McCord greeted the Officer of the Deck with a genial, "good morning," and went over to study the chart and check the log. Everything ship-shape. "Morning, Morgan," he said to the giant quartermaster at the wheel.

"Morning, sir," the veteran sailor rumbled.

McCord stepped out on the wing of the bridge, as the Admiral had done, and noted the spotted planes, and looked up at the direction of the white caps on the water. A moderate sea was running, lifting the bow and letting it fall back in a nice rhythm, with no roll. She was doing just fine. San Francisco, we're on our way.

The next day was Sunday. Not that Sunday means much in a combat zone; you can't trust the enemy to take a breather just because your culture believes that God made the world in six days and rested on the seventh. The area in the bow adjoining the forward elevator was the designated chapel and on Sundays it was as busy as a bus station. The Catholic chaplain had it first with an early mass. Then came the Protestants in a Baptist service. Every other Sunday the Episcopal minister held forth—usually to smaller congregations. Today all services were jammed. The imminence of battle had inspired a lot of soul-searching.

The other good thing about this Sunday was letters from home. "Mail call" was by all odds the most appreciated summons that ever crackled through the ship. I got a letter from Maggie. Blue. Smelling of perfume.

Mike my darling,

Enough's enough. The papers are full of rumors about a huge force taking back the Philippines. Surely this means this war's about to end. Why don't you simply take credit for winning and come on home while you've got one, Slim. Your daughters will be delighted to have a war hero for a father and I'll be proud to go to church with an escort. There may be other reasons why I'd enjoy having you home but I can no longer remember. Perhaps you can refresh me.

Good news. The sailor and his motorcycle are gone. Perhaps embarked out there with you.

I do miss you, darling. *Come home.*

Love,

Maggie

The Admiral was restless. A day of recuperation may be all right for the fliers and their aircraft, but he wanted to get on with the war. The grand design for the invasion was all in place. What was MacArthur waiting for?

The old man paced the flag bridge impatiently, talking with me and Stowell, asking questions, going inside to study charts, smoking, pacing, staring at the sea.

On the hangar deck it was business as usual. Planes were being repaired, motors tuned, plugs replaced, fuel lines blown out, and bullet holes plugged. The huge maintenance crew that kept the Air Group flying was busy getting ready for the next one. The noise was deafening. Electric saws whined. Riveting machines stuttered. Hammers banged. Engines sputtered. And the smell of gas and oil hung over it all like the scent of roses over an English garden.

I accompanied Fritz to his plane on the hangar deck. Panetta, his plane chief, was on a ladder—as usual, with his head buried in the engine. "How's she looking, Joe?" Fritz called. Panetta's face, faintly smudged with oil, emerged grinning. "She'll do, Commander, but you got some bullet holes."

"I was lucky."

"Lucky ain't the word, Commander. Like Swiss cheese!"

"That bad?"

"Worse. Only thing saved you, your crew chief's Italian—same as the Lord."

Fritz chuckled. The rest of his crew, Monk and Lafferty, were working on the wings. One was in the cockpit; the other was under the plane calling out instructions. "Okay, sir," Monk called down from the cockpit. "You nearly lost an aileron, Commander," Lafferty said.

"Thanks for catching it," Fritz said.

"No problem," Monk said.

Back in his quarters Fritz, wearing a broad grin, tossed me the latest letter from his son.

Salisbury Academy

Hello Dad:

Thanks for the check! Boy, do I need it!

My roommate and I went to Washington last Saturday and threw money around like J.P. Morgan. We took two girls to the movies and afterwards went to Harvey's where they ate like pigs. Not only lobsters but dessert. You wouldn't believe two small females could put away so much! I didn't do too bad myself, but I nearly lost it all when the bill came. Harry said to the waiter, 'We just came for dinner. We didn't want to buy the place.'

The girls panicked at that, though it wasn't original.

It's pretty exciting having a father on a carrier. Harry's dad is some kind of 4-F. I think Harry's embarrassed, but the poor old guy had some kind of heart condition so what could he do?

Mom stopped bringing her new beau to the school -- thank God! She looks real thin and smokes a lot. Asks me if I've heard from you and how you are. I guess you're fine. That's what I tell her anyhow. Got to stop now as tomorrow is a Latin test and I haven't got the faintest notion what that crazy Caesar is up to. Thanks for the do-re-mi.

Give 'em hell, Dad.

Love,
Tom

As evening came, the Admiral attended the Episcopal service. When he returned to the bridge he seemed to be in a pensive mood. Did he have a sense of huge forces gathering in the wings for imminent action on a large scale? I knew he was eager to start, but what about the thousands who would die? That must be bothering the hell out of him. I didn't envy him the job.

The old man leaned over the outer edge of the flag bridge, apparently savoring the sight of the ship cutting through the sea screened by destroyers against subs, with more destroyers and cruisers in an anti-aircraft ring halfway to the horizon—all under his command. I wondered if, like every plebe at Annapolis, he had dreamed of such a moment? As I watched, a gooney bird cruised past the carrier barely clearing the small waves. A dozen gulls swung back and forth in the ship's boiling wake searching for tidbits. From the forward elevator came the sounds of an organ and a hymn. The sun was setting. It was a peaceful evening. I thought about Maggie's letter; and yearned to reread it in private. Finally, I dragged into my cabin, kicked off the boots and turned on the reading light over the bed. My glasses were clouded with salt spray. Rather than get up and clean them, I dug out my "back-up specs," as Fritz called them, and picked up the letter, giving it a good sniff before beginning.

She was right. We were going to win this thing. Why not get it over and go home? Tell that to the Marines. Those presently seasick warriors trained to take the high ground, to wade ashore under heavy fire; a bunch of eager kids playing soldier with live ammo.

I couldn't go home yet. Not while the ship was heavily committed to the invasion. Not while the Admiral needed an ACI.

"Bullshit," is what Maggie would say to this—being a candid young woman who rarely used obscenities but snapped them out when she thought they were necessary.

# Twenty-one

*Contemptible fly lands*
*on ready room ceiling*
*upside down. Aviator!*

Niki Osaka hated his commander. At sixteen Niki was a smart, smiling, fun-loving boy who didn't like to be yelled at. The Commander yelled all the time. He had a quite accurate notion that Niki was a much smarter man than he seemed. When Niki volunteered to join the Army, it was against his mother's wishes. Not that Niki was all that patriotic; he loved his father and his brothers, but life seemed to be too serious with them. He wasn't ready for this war. He joined more in rebellion against his family than any sudden patriotism.

Now he was sorry. His Commander was a stupid colonel who thought the way to teach young recruits to fly was to make them more afraid of him than of the threatening mysteries of flight. The Army now was attempting to develop a kamikaze corps like the Navy. There was, however, a major difference. Admiral Onishi's fliers were volunteers. Colonel Butto's men were ordered to volunteer.

Niki knew he couldn't postpone his solo flight any longer. He joined those of his group who said they were ready. Butto sent them up like young horses on a lead, taking a jump for the first time. One crashed and killed himself. The Colonel was infuriated; if the boy hadn't died in the crash, no doubt the Colonel would have shot him. Two others passed, one failed, returning to earth in a wobbly fashion and nearly running over the Colonel. Another tantrum.

When Niki's time came he made a smooth takeoff and pulled up over the trees in fine style. He felt like a great bird. Below he could see the women in the wet fields, the water buffaloes pulling the ancient plow. He pulled back on the stick and the Zero rose like a hawk, its red spots gleaming. Niki had an impulse to head north and forget the Colonel and all his words. Not yet. Too soon for that. Just wait. The time would come.

Niki put the fighter through its paces, turning, falling, climbing, pretending an enemy was on top of him. It was all very easy and Niki could tell that he was a natural. Don't let the Colonel know. Screw it up a little.

He came in fast—just for the Colonel—bounced twice and swerved around sharply as he used a single break.

"What are you trying to do?" the Colonel yelled.

"Sorry, sir," Niki said, climbing down. He knew he'd made it.

Niki loved Ken and Miro and was proud when the older brothers had become part of the Navy. Ken and Miro had emulated their father all their lives, so it seemed natural for them to volunteer. Niki had always been a gentle rebel, not wanting to follow the pattern, yet not wanting to hurt his parents with outright disobedience. This ambivalence had gotten him caught by Army Air and—almost before he realized it—he was part of something he hated and was secretly determined to get out of— a secret he'd shared with his friend the grocer's son. As they whispered together during rainy nights at the encampment, a plan began to develop. The other boy's accident had disrupted their plans, but had increased Niki's determination to make his escape.

He took every opportunity to study charts of the islands, memorizing landing fields and defensive positions. Once his solo flight was completed, Niki knew he'd have to anticipate movement to forward areas. The Colonel seemed to grow more abusive as the group neared the end of their training. Niki tried to stay alert for the first indications of deployment and, sure enough, they weren't long in coming. Another Colonel, wearing wings, turned up and made a long talk pointing out the essential elements of the kamikaze attack. He ended by bowing to them as a group and congratulated them on "volunteering." Had he been more perceptive, he might have wondered whether the sullen silence of his reception might have indicated a morale problem. But, having done what he flew down there to do, he clicked his heels, bowed again and flew away.

# Twenty-two

Joining up above their carrier, the *Sussex* fliers formed their attack pattern and headed west with the sun still well below the horizon. Like their Admiral they saw the vast armada moving towards the land and inevitably must have felt proud to be part of it.

*Sussex*, with smoke trailing straight back over her white wake, was flanked on the left by *Charleston,* on the right by *Gettysburg*; from their decks also rose a stream of planes forming up and heading west. Behind each carrier steamed two destroyers, ready to pick up ditched fliers. Ahead rode the submarine guards—two more lean grey ships with white moustaches at their plunging bows.

Ahead of the carriers were the heavy cruisers; also flanked by destroyers and in the midst of the cruisers the great battleship *New Mexico,* broad-beamed, massive, threatening.

Far to the left and far to the right other carriers, cruisers and destroyers moved toward the big islands.

Surrounded on all sides within this wall of ships were the fat, crowded troop transports attended by landing craft.

It seemed to me as if all the ships and planes in the world must be assembled in this massive force. Surely the Japs would give up and let everybody go home; or would they? I wondered. If it took this many vessels, planes and men to attack, what must the Japs have in defense? With years to prepare for the American assault what ugly reception had they prepared? I was glad that I wasn't a Marine about to set foot on those sandy beaches under Japanese gunfire.

As Fritz later reported it, he felt fine. Terry was back where he belonged, flying wing. Getting that scoundrel back just about made his day.

"Don't I get a Purple Heart for being bitten by the enemy?" Terry had said, making everybody laugh. He had a picture of the baby, plus a wonderful letter from Tony, so why worry about the Japs? The size of the armada headed for the Philippines added to his mood. This had to be the assault that would make them realize they couldn't win. Like Fritz he said he was awed by the size of the force and proud to be a part of it. The rescue gave him an added feeling of hope; he was back where he belonged, in the air; the Japs had their chance to kill him and they'd failed. From now on they couldn't touch him.

In exactly fifty minutes, just as we had promised, the first of the islands rose out of the early morning mist. Automatically checking his altitude and fuel, Fritz wondered how he was going to hit anything if the mist didn't dissipate. It was all very well to show recon photos taken in bright sunlight, but what he had at the moment was cone-shaped mountaintops touched with the gold of a rising sun. Very appropriate. It wasn't their homeland but near enough. What do we do now?

An early rising trade wind answered the question for him by brushing away the mist and revealing the targets, freshly washed, nestled among the greens and tans of the Philippine Islands. He checked his chart, took a quick glance at the recon photos, located the AA gun positions and pushed over into his dive. Under his wings were two fragmentation bombs. As always the presence of danger increased his pulse, dried up his mouth, sharpened his sight, made him unaccountably eager. The dive itself was thrilling; the total absence of flak made it even more so. Just at the end, before he had to pull out, he saw men running to the guns and removing camouflage netting. "Thanks, gentlemen," he murmured and released his bombs squarely on target. Behind him Terry came screaming down and struck the next gun.

The rest of the huge flight followed, striking barracks, radio stations, bridges, ammo dumps, parked tanks, cargo planes. The Japanese knew the invasion was beginning and they were ready. They knew that the day would bring the heavy shells from battleships and cruisers and then the troops. Thousands upon thousands of Marines coming ashore and spreading across the island. In tanks, in half tracks, on foot running and firing. The Americans were coming ashore and there was no way to stop them, but—for the Emperor's sake—they could try. Their defenses were in depth, and they would fight to the last man.

Rawlings reported that he stayed as long as his fuel gauge would allow, directing the attacks of his divebombers, strafing targets of opportunity. When the time came for his group to return to the carrier, he brought up the rear with Terry, having noted the loss of two aircraft, both of which had headed out to sea, trailing smoke. Fritz saw neither plane on the way back, hoping they'd made it, realizing they were probably in the drink.

As I listened to Fritz describe the target island so green and luscious I thought about a holiday with Maggie when we were based in San Diego. We had sent the girls to grandparents and had gone to San Miguel d'Allende, four hours north of Mexico City. We stayed in a hotel called the Instituto where the floors were red tile and the lawns outside were cut by squatting Indians using hand sickles. There seemed to be chickens and children everywhere, each group with its own sound. The children laughing, the chickens cackling. The days were hot and lazy; with strolls through cobblestone streets to the vegetable markets and leather and silver shops; with siestas and love-making. The nights were noisy, with guitar music near and far and sad-sounding songs. Through the louvered doors of our large room we heard the loud click of heels in the corridor. From outside we could hear the sporadic braying of the burros, whose long wailing hee-haws seemed to be a litany of protest against the burdensome lives they led. When the human sounds finally died, the tiny burros still cried out, though no one was listening except sleepy birds who now and then called back. The air was cool and smelled of pungent wood smoke from the cook fires of Indian families living on every side of the hotel in old stone and adobe houses.

Maggie was sensitive to the sounds and smells, bringing them to my attention as if she were a birdwatcher hearing the call of a new warbler. She was in a wonderful holiday mood, I remembered, frisky and playful, enjoying the frolic of foreplay, often bubbling with laughter as my mouth closed over hers. I fell asleep smiling.

Up early aboard *Sussex* I collected a cup of coffee and found my way to the nearest fresh air and view of the sea—in a gun tub just below the flight deck. My only companion was a young Marine attending a twin-barreled 40 mm anti-aircraft weapon. We were both yawning. I offered him a swallow, he accepted gratefully. It was not chit-chat time; we were both still half asleep. Every inch of exposed metal on the gun gleamed in the early sunlight. I got the feeling that, whatever may happen, this young man and this polished instrument would do their part. "Have another swallow of coffee."

I was keenly aware of being only a tiny unit in the living organism that was the ship. In concept, the carrier was an ocean-going platform on which bullet-firing and bomb-carrying aircraft could take off and land. In reality, it was a teeming city-at-sea. Not a democratic city, to be sure; rather a benign dictatorship. The Captain—for all his good manners—had the final word on what everybody did—except for an old man with three stars on his collar.

I was still a relative outsider among all these naval types—in spite of months on the job. I was an observer, not a true citizen of the city. The elite, of course, were the fliers. Everybody who wasn't a flier, was there to serve them, to get them within range of a target. "Everybody" included the Captain, the chief engineer, the barber, even the ACI officer and the kid on the shining anti-aircraft gun.

If the Captain wanted us to abandon ship, we would do so. If the Captain wanted the fliers to dine with him, they did so. If the Captain wanted brandy to be served—it was "down the hatches." If he wanted me to jump overboard—"so long folks."

I cherished this unusually peaceful morning at sea. It was still early enough to be cool. Also, being on the starboard side and heading southwest, we were half-screened from the early sun. Dolphins picked us up and paced our anti-sub destroyers—in and out of the dark water their wet skin burnished by the sun. Floating branches told us we were near land, as did strange birds circling over our wake. I wondered how the ocean life felt about this huge racing shadow with its spinning propellers and generous garbage.

My young Marine friend was Jimmy Ball, "from New Orleans."

"A great city."

"Yes, sir."

"Ever eat at Simpsons?" A stupid question.

"No, sir. Too expensive."

"No matter where you go, food's great."

"Right, sir."

"Ever take that old side-wheeler?" Second stupid question.

"No, sir. That's for tourists."

"How about she-crab soup? Where do you get that?" A desperate try.

"Home. My mom makes it great."

"Imagine! She-crab soup at home."

"Yes, sir."

I knew what lay ahead of us on the islands in our southwesterly path. The very antithesis of early morning serenity: bombings, strafings, explosions, men wading ashore with rifles held high, men dying as aircraft rounds stitched their way across the sand, sewing young soldiers into the deadly beach.

I shook my head and finished off my coffee. Whatever was ahead, I might as well shave my one-eyed face. "Good luck, Jimmy."

"Thank you, sir."


Our invading armada was closer to the target. *New Mexico* was pouring shells ashore. So were the cruisers. The troopships were getting ready to put people over the side in nets, to be packed into landing vehicles and carried to the beach under heavy defensive fire. Rawlings and his bombers had done their best to cut down such fire, as the heavy guns offshore were also doing. But he knew the landing would be costly and he was glad he wasn't in a Marine assault unit wading ashore through the surf.

Captain McCord was happy. I never saw him in a better mood. Everything was in place and functioning smoothly. The lee helm had just passed an order to the engine room. The Officer of the Deck had just confirmed a relative position with the navigator. The junior officer of the deck had just brought the Captain's binoculars from his sea cabin. Both talkers, with earphones, had just been in touch with distant parts of the ship. One had located the XO and asked him to come to the bridge; the other had taken a message from the air boss that the last plane was back from the strike. The Officer of the Deck had just altered the course of the ship; she had been going straight into the wind. Now she could ease off a few points. This was the way the Navy was supposed to be: orderly, efficient, according to the book.

In the same mood the *Sussex* flight came back so smoothly, landed so routinely with remarkably little battle damage. Some of the planes had shrapnel scars or machine gun punctures. The two missing planes had not reached the ship, so we could only pray that somebody had seen them or that they made an alternative landing. No word so far.

The incoming planes were spotted forward, waiting to be taken to the hangar deck, repaired where necessary, refueled and made ready for a second flight according to the Op plan. The forward elevator was functioning perfectly. In record time it had taken almost half the planes below for servicing and rearming. In anticipation, the armament team had worked diligently since before daybreak bringing up bombs and ammo from below to pre-position for the restrike.

As the pilots jumped out of their aircraft they ran for the head, then reported to the ready room for debriefing. Some sought out the wardroom for a second breakfast. A few went to their cabins. It was not yet eleven-hundred-thirty. The heat lay over the ship in a smothering cloud. On the flag bridge the Admiral was listening to reports from his fleet. Everything was proceeding according to plan. Stowell was busy with dispatches. The Admiral took time out to open and read a letter from his wife. He chuckled as he read it and handed it to me.

Dear Dan,

Did you know somebody wrote a piece about you in *Time* Magazine? I can't imagine where they got their information. It certainly didn't sound like you. More like a movie actor or a politician. They simply shouldn't print things like that without checking with a person. Here's a sample:

"Tall, sea-seasoned Dan Duncan, three-star Admiral wearing a salty long-billed baseball cap, closed one piercing blue eye and grinned as he threw down the gauntlet to Japanese Emperor, Hirohito..." and so forth.

Made you sound *just plain silly* and I don't believe you said it.

Miss you more than ever. I get the feeling we're winning the war and I hope and pray I'm right. To prove how much I miss you right this minute, I actually wouldn't make the slightest fuss if you left your wading boots in the front hall, smoked your pipe in the bedroom, or tried to kiss me with a beard after a three-day hunting trip. What more can a man ask?
Love,
Emma
P.S. The Garden Club elected me president. Does that outrank Admiral? I think it does.

I had my own letter.

Mike Darling,

All of us here on the home front know that you have won the war. But nobody has told the Japs. If any of the Imperial high command read *Time* magazine, he'd know that he can't win. Why don't you send one of those hotshot pilots like Fritz over there and drop a leaflet? You better do something soon. I've had it with solitary spouse-hood. I love you—no doubt about that—but I've forgotten what you look like. Short, fat, redhead?

Your daughters think you're tall, dark and handsome. Please reconcile these domestic differences. And come home while I still remember your name, Billy Boy.
Mine is,
Maggie

Above us on his own bridge the Captain watched his fliers return with satisfaction. Hearing of the missing pilots, he shook his head and said a prayer. Surely they'd be picked up by an armada this big. Otherwise, for the moment all was well. *Sussex* had done her share, sent her planes, struck her targets, retrieved all but three, and was preparing to live up to her commitment with a second flight at fourteen-hundred.

Below him four decks down in CIC, men were watching a screen on which green blips represented planes and ships as the radar scope swept in a circle like a giant windshield wiper. Somebody must have said, "What the hell is that?" A fast-moving blip was closing with the ship.

"No IFF. It's a bogey."

A phone rang on the bridge.

"This is the Captain."

"Sir, we've got a bogey closing at 250 knots vector 145."

The Captain spoke quickly into another phone, "General Quarters. General Quarters. Incoming bogey off starboard beam—fire when ready."

The Admiral heard the alarm and strode to the other side of his bridge, using his binocs. He picked up the plane flying low—a Japanese light bomber called a Betty. Was the pilot crazy? *Sussex* shell bursts were all around him. Water spouts jumped up everywhere and still he didn't waver. A sudden chill came over us. This was a kamikaze. This was who sank Princeton and the others.

"If we don't hit him, he's coming aboard," the old man said quietly.

I ran up the ladder three at a time. There was McCord watching the near misses of his anti-aircraft guns pointing almost level with the sea; he struck the rail of his bridge with a closed fist and growled, "Come on, boys—stop the sonofabitch!" In a matter of seconds we knew it was too late. *Sussex* was about to be hit by a suicide pilot with a plane load of bombs and there was nothing we could do about it.

# Twenty-three

*Farewell, climbing rose*
*singing lark, house cricket, Mount Fuji*
*Old rain, don't weep.*

Ensign Osaka knew it was his last night on earth. He couldn't sleep. He lay wide-eyed, staring at the corrugated roof and listening to the eternal rain, the birds, the repair shops. The thought of his father suffocated him. Again and again he saw the blue planes diving, firing, bombing. He imagined his father alone on the bridge shaking a fist at them; tomorrow they'd get more than a shaken fist. He'd pick the biggest carrier he could find and slam into her island. He'd carry his bomb into the Captain's quarters and shove it down his throat or, if he could find an open elevator shaft, he'd take his message to the loading aircraft where the gasoline would do its worst.

Four more hours. He was angry, with a passion that changed the quiet sensitive boy into a man with a mission. He decided he would not tell the Lieutenant Commander. He didn't want to risk having him say, "Better wait. You're too valuable to waste as a kamikaze." Too late for that now. Too late for everything.

His resolve gradually faded and he thought of summers on his grandfather's farm when he and Miro and Niki were boys. He remembered jumping from the roof of the barn and landing in the haystack -- a wonderful landing, in sweet smelling hay, soft, as if he were being embraced. At first Niki was afraid, but when he saw how easy it was, with no harm done, he had jumped too. All night the three of them had sneezed from the dust of the haystack.

What happens to you, little brother? Will you, too, be diving on an enemy ship to avenge our father? Don't do it, Niki. One is enough.

Almost irreverently the face of a girl came to him out of the darkness. Going to be a doctor. They stand together now, holding hands. They're at the window of her apartment and her breasts are bare. He kisses them and she holds his head against her breast. He takes her in his arms and they make love on the bed.

Ken thought back. Only a year ago Tiko and he had first fallen in love. She was a medical student at Tokyo University. He had just graduated from the naval college. Their parents were friends, her father also a senior naval officer. The last day they were together was one of the nicest days Ken could remember. His father, miraculously on leave from his precious *Amato*, had decided to take the young couple, plus Niki, then aged fourteen, for a long sail on the family schooner, which Ken and Niki had worked hard to get ready, airing out the mildewed sails, trying the engine in case it was needed, while their mother supervised a great lunch with help in the kitchen.

As they chugged away from the dock in the tidal river where they'd built their summer house, Captain Osaka was at the wheel, looking very nautical in his blue yachting cap and open-throat shirt. Both boys outdid themselves as lively deckhands, leaping about, coiling unused lines in nice neat circles, fetching cups of tea to their mother and Tiko, and addressing their father, in mock and affectionate deference, as "Captain." With sunny skies and a good breeze the little schooner had put forth her wings like a graceful bird and carried them pleasantly out of the mouth of their tidal river and across a stretch of open water to reach a landfall at a small island where they dropped anchor and ate their lunch. Though it was still early spring both boys had defied the cold and dived overboard in their bathing suits — to be followed quickly by Tiko in spite of their shouts of discomfort. All three had then swum ashore and raced down the beach. Their father, putting the dingy overboard, had sculled it ashore loaded with large terry cloth towels, which were most gratefully received.

That night, in the faint light of a new moon, Ken and Tiko had walked down the dock where the schooner was tied up. Standing at the dock's end, listening to the slap of small waves, and the bump of the schooner against the pilings, Ken had put his arms around her and she had turned her face up for his kiss. His mind had been full of thoughts, half sentences, and passionate words but all he could manage when they paused for breath was "Tiko." They had kissed again and she had made no move to remove his hands as they crept over her breasts. Nor did she protest when he led her aboard the schooner and down into the cabin where the bunks were. There on the slightly mildewed covers of a bunk they had made love, hesitant at first, then deeply satisfying.

In the bright light of morning, embarked in an aircraft from which he knew he would never emerge, Ken clung to the memory of the night on the sailboat with Tiko and was filled with an overwhelming sense of sadness. His desire to avenge his father wavered in the face of his sadness—the face of Tiko, pale and beautiful in the cabin of the schooner. A face that now floated between him and the dials of the plane, pleading; he could almost hear the sound of her voice saying, "Don't do this. Don't end your life. Stay alive—with me."

He shook his head, as if to clear away such dangerous thoughts, and forced himself to look at airspeed, 130 knots; petrol, half-full; oil, low. Below him—blue water, and further back, green islands where rice grew in paddies and old men drove ox carts. *Where were Miro and little Niki?*

*Too late. Wait for me, Father. I'm on my way.*

# Twenty-four

*Small bird at cannon's mouth*
*peers inside. "What a lovely*
*spot to build a nest."*

Ensign Osaka, from high above anti-aircraft range, reigned as lord of the universe. At that height the earth seemed remote and breathing was hard. Below, the sea looked flat and metalic dotted with toy ships. A cluster of toys moved west toward the islands. Escort carriers only—plus destroyers and a troop ship. They acknowledged his presence; sending up black shellbursts far below, more a salute than a threat. He knew what he wanted:  To kill an *Essex* class carrier—the ultimate symbol of American power. Let somebody else dive into the smaller carriers, his goal was the biggest one.

He checked his fuel again. Getting very low. Last thing he'd want was to run out and have to dive into the nearest ship—and, incidentally inflict less damage. His throat began to feel dry. His head ached, and for a moment or two he surveyed his chart, as a feeling of desperation began to overtake him, the thrill of his take-off wearing away. The original kamikaze concept carried with it a religious feeling of imperviousness. It had seemed to be an almost mystical state—in which the act of bravery and suicide were transitions to a more exalted state. This elation was fading; replacing it were the pressure of his headache, the mounting desperation of the unsuccessful hunt. Would his father be proud of him? His father was dead. His mother?  She wouldn't say so, but she would disapprove. She did not believe in the masculine military world but rarely spoke out.

He dropped down into a thick cloud. For a last cool white moment he was alone with his thoughts. Then he burst out into the blazing sunshine and there she was—an *Essex* class carrier with planes on deck.

Almost immediately he had company—two F6Fs closing fast. Combat air patrol doing its duty above the fleet. He pushed over and began his dive. They followed, overtaking and stitching .50 calibers along his fuselage. No hope to evade them. Just hang on, dodging and turning, make sure not to get blown off course.

He was closing fast. The other kamikazes were spotting their own targets. *Sussex* was protected like a queen bee. Coming in low, the way the old Admiral said. A monster ship! Shellbursts everywhere. Ahead, above, behind, close. Ensign Osaka pulled back on the stick and the Betty jumped almost straight up, giving him a side view. Forward elevator was down. He kicked to the right as he rose over the carrier. Time seemed to slow down. He felt a shell strike. He saw men running. He heard the scream of his engine. He felt the first millisecond of the bomb's force. Heard the universe explode. Sun, sea and sky turned to fire.

# Twenty-five

$J$ust before it reached the carrier, the incoming plane rose sharply, as if to swoop across the flight deck. Then it dove into the open shaft of the forward elevator and exploded among the partially loaded aircraft, among the piles and rows of bombs, among the gasoline pumps, among the men. It exploded in a mass of burning gasoline and red hot bomb fragments. The concussive force flattened all obstacles and personnel for hundreds of yards, and burst upwards in a release of terrible force. Standing with the Captain, I was hurled against the bulkhead as the blast shattered the glass of the bridge. The Captain was down, almost on top of me, holding his hands over his bleeding face. Finding it difficult to see, I realized that my glasses had been shattered, leaving me almost blind.

When the Captain's hands came away from his face, they were bloody. Leaning close and squinting, I could tell that there were cuts on his forehead and cheek, but both eyes seemed okay. Together we struggled to our feet and the Captain brushed himself off and took command. "Bosun," the Captain spoke calmly.

"Aye, sir?"

"Fire in the hangar deck. Get on the pipe."

"Yes, sir!"

Starting with the klaxon, the announcement rang through the ship. "General Quarters! General Quarters!" Then, "Fire! Fire! Fire! Fire! Hangar deck frames number one and two. Man all fire stations."

There was a second explosion, then a third. Flames and smoke boiled up out of the elevator shaft. The smoke, black and smelling of gasoline and cordite, swept aft to the bridge. Heavy concussions shook the ship, as refueled planes caught fire and exploded. Ammunition began going off like intermittent gunfire.

When the first announcement was over, McCord took the microphone. In a quiet voice he said, "This is the Captain. An enemy plane has hit the hangar deck. Forward elevator. Damage control report on the double. Hospital personnel prepare for casualties. Medics to the hangar deck on the double. Medics to the hangar deck on the double."

He snapped off the microphone in fury. *Sussex* was on fire. His *Sussex*. His beautiful ship would have no further participation in the great battle. I'm sure his immediate concern was his men. God knows how many were dead, how many more would die. Bombs were still exploding; *Sussex herself might not survive.*

"Ease her off five points," he said to the helmsman, "that'll take the smoke out of our face."

"Aye, sir—five points it is."

The Admiral, in the direct path of the thick smoke, must have been glad when the ship changed course and the smoke shot off to the right. As deeply concerned as he was about *Sussex*, he had other ships to worry about—"More ships than I can count," he'd recently told Stowell. From the look of things, my guess was he'd be moving his flag. But where? Our dispatches reported *Gettysburg* had taken a kamikaze hit and was afire. The cruiser *Richmond* had taken one on the bridge, killing her captain and putting her temporarily out of control. *Shenandoah* had a narrow miss, having shot down its kamikaze at the last second.

Once again intelligence had been right as they had been right—oh, so right—about Midway. Japan's last ditch defense was the suiciders, and every ship in the American Pacific fleet was vulnerable to planes that didn't have to turn back at the limit of fuel range, that were flown by pilots who were ready to take incredible risks for the simple reason that they didn't expect to return home alive. We had been dreading such a weapon and the terrible threat it posed.

The Captain helped his quartermaster to his feet. "I'm okay, sir," the older sailor said in deep tones as he resumed his place at the wheel. I knew I'd be useless without my glasses, so—with the Captain's permission, I set out for my cabin to get my "spare specs," without which I was about as helpful as a blind mule. It was not an easy journey, all passageways and ladders were clogged with sailors, pilots, non-coms, and officers on their way to battle stations, or merely heading topside to get away from the fires.

Two young sailors shoved me off a ladder yelling, "Coming through, mister." As I reached out and grabbed the foot of one sailor, his buddy struck me in the face. I yanked the sailor off the ladder and slammed him against his buddy. "Calm down, you little bastards," I growled. I could barely make out their faces—a fact, fortunately, they were unaware of. They called off the contest and scrambled up the ladder like monkeys.

I continued my salmon-swimming-upstream efforts to reach my cabin, narrowly avoiding a second confrontation at a watertight door with a huge non-com who came through like the evening mail, brushing aside all living creatures on his headlong rush to some place, coughing and choking in the dark and smoke-filled passage. I continued the journey. When I reached my cabin, literally clawing my way for the last fifty yards, I banged the door shut and went to the wash basin. One squint in the mirror and I couldn't restrain a twisted grin. Christ, what a mess! I had more cuts from the glass splinters than I realized. I looked like a creature from hell, with blood caked on both cheeks and a slash across the forehead. I washed my face, wincing over as the water stung the scratches. Then I wiped my face and put on my glasses. What a relief! No time to linger. From the size of the explosions we could be losing the ship. I grabbed the blue letter, stuffed it in my trousers, and reentered the desperate parade in the passages. It was easier going with the tide.

Badly winded from running down passageways and ladders, I reached the hangar deck about twenty minutes after the Japanese plane hit. As I pushed open a heavy hatch, and stepped inside, the noise hit me like a blow in the face. At the far end, where the elevator had been, a fire roared, with flames shooting upwards as if the elevator shaft were a giant chimney. As I started forward, a plane exploded near the fire, blinding me with its sudden flame, tearing my sleeve with a fragment of hot metal. I was stunned for a moment, and terrified. Why was I here? What could I do? Above the roar of the flames I could hear men screaming, men wounded by the exploding bombs, men saturated with flaming gasoline, men stumbling in a daze from the force of the explosions. Then I came upon men dead from the first blast, naked against the bulkhead, their clothes blown off, their bodies seared. Out of the smoke I saw Fritz with three sailors dragging bombs away from a stream of flaming gasoline. I ran toward them.

"Mike!" he called out. "Lend us a hand." I joined them and we moved the bombs and then put our shoulders against an armed aircraft, gradually pushing it overboard. One of the men recognized Fritz. "What are you doing here, Mr. Rawlings?"

"Looking for Panetta. You seen him?"

The man's expression darkened. "He was near the elevator when the fuckin' Jap hit us. Nothing left of him. Buddy of mine saw it happen."

Rawlings steadied himself against the fuselage of the plane, where six Japanese flags had been painted in celebration of its pilot's combat success. Little Joe who was always kidding about having a safe job while Fritz and the others were being shot at. I felt sick. "What about Monk and Lafferty?"

"They was with Joe, sir."

The reply was apologetic. Rawlings breathed deep, then stepped forward to help disengage the bomb. I joined him, fighting nausea. As we embraced the bomb I thought of its awful force and shuddered to think how many of them had been dropped. Very strongly I felt the closeness of death. Twenty feet away lay the bodies of men killed in the first explosion, irrelevant now, no longer part of the "mighty invasion." Fritz quickly appraised the situation. Two planes near the fire had already blown up. Three others were smoking, with small flames beginning to show on the wings of fuselage. The bulk of the planes lay within the fire's reach. Something had to be done. We needed all the help we could get.

"You on the tractor!  Move it forward and get those aircraft away from the fire."

Nevitt stared at Fritz, who shouted, "Haul 'em away from the fire before they blow up. Get going."

Clearing his throat, Ben managed, "Okay, sir." He started the tractor engine and reached out to touch the dashboard, as if he were reassuring a horse that everything would be all right. Taking a deep breath, he put the tractor into gear and drove slowly toward the fire, the bombs, and the yelling men and burning aircraft.

Fritz saw the look on Ben's face, hopped on the back of the tractor and put his hand on the boy's shoulder. In a calm voice he said, "All right, son, take it easy. Straight ahead."

Ben swallowed and murmured, "Sure." Was the man crazy? The plane was on *fire!*

Reading his mind, Fritz patted Ben's shoulder, "If we move fast, we'll be okay."

"Jesus!" Ben said, "If?"

Noting that the tractor was equipped for pushing with a bulldozer type of blade made of wood, Fritz pointed to a gaping hole blown in the side of the ship by the Japanese bombs. "Shove her overboard, son. Right through there."

Ben shifted gears, quickly turned to put the bulldozer blade against the plane's tail and slowly let out the clutch. The tractor made contact; the burning plane moved. Twice Rawlings and I yanked the tail around when it didn't seem to be headed right. The heat was intense, bitter with the smell of gasoline, paint and melting aluminum.

"Shove her hard!" Rawlings yelled, shielding his face from the heat. Ben held his breath, stepped on the gas, moved the TBM to the huge gaping hole in the ship's side. As soon as the engine passed through the opening the tail tipped up and—much to Ben's relief—the whole aircraft flipped over the side, exploding just as it reached the water. All of us heard the gas tank go.

"Okay, son, good work. Now let's get that one."

Rawlings pointed to a Hellcat that was starting to burn.

I knew that I couldn't take much more. It was Dante's inferno come to life—or death. Maybe a place to read about in an epic poem or a novel, but not a place to be in person. Yet I was committed to it and Fritz needed all the help he could get. At this point a very large pair of shoulders appeared through the smoke. Looking for Rawlings, Terry Vernon had stepped inside the hangar deck and was now in smoke that burned his eyes and choked his windpipe. As his vision cleared, he ran forward at a jog, and saw us—me, Fritz, working with Ben Nevitt and the tractor. Together we were pushing a burning Hellcat toward a jagged hole in the ship's side. Fritz greeted Terry with a quick grin, his teeth suddenly white in a blackened face. "Hey, Terry, lend us a hand, old man."

By now Fritz's shirt and trousers had scorched spots and an ugly scratch ran down his left forearm. He pointed to a row of parked planes in the path of the advancing flames. "Those have got to be moved."

Terry yelled, "You bet," and grabbed three partially dazed sailors shouting, "Follow me."

As the four of them reached the line of planes, Terry took charge. "Okay, roll 'em." He ducked under the wings and kicked out the chocks, removed the last tie-downs; then the three crewmen put their weight against the fuselage. Slowly, the torpecker began to roll. It was hard to believe that anything so heavy could fly. One of the crewmen—a swarthy youngster—broke away from the group, muttering, "Fuck this." Terry reached out and grabbed him.

"Take it easy, sailor. We need you."

The youngster looked at Terry in fury. "I gotta get outa here. This whole fucking deck is going to blow."

"Horseshit," Terry yelled. "The worst is over. Stick with me, boy."

The sailor stared at Terry, opening and closing his fists. I put a hand on the youngster's shoulder. "Come on, son. Do what the man says."

Muttering, the kid fell back in line, added his weight to the push. We tried not to look at the terrible dead as the plane moved past them.

The central core of the fire—the Japanese plane—had consumed itself. Its bombs had done their worst, its fuel was gone, its wings and fuselage turned into white ashes, and its pilot incinerated. I wondered if he was smiling down on us from his Emperor's garden?

The surrounding areas had become littered with broken aircraft, fragments of wings, tails, canopies, parts of fuselage, landing gear.

Standing in the midst of all this were the asbestos-suited firefighters, covered with foam, struggling with hoses, slipping and sliding on the steel deck, sick at heart and nauseated by what they had seen. Among the men, wearing an open asbestos jacket, was the XO, directing, encouraging, sympathizing, bullying, cursing, patting backs, lifting bodies. By now his shirt had been torn, his face cut, his hands were burned, and his left knee could be seen through his torn trouser leg. This was his job, his men, his ship.

Working hard, we managed to separate the useful planes from the approaching fire and dump the burning planes overboard. There they fell crackling and sometimes scraping against the carrier's hull, sometimes exploding on impact with the water. A long time later the fire-control men apparently stopped the flames from spreading in our direction. We were exhausted and running with sweat.

When he thought we'd done all we could do with the planes, Fritz grabbed me and yelled, "We better check below." Gasping, I followed him into smoking passageways, exhausted and sick at my stomach. Our progress was slow. We had to struggle against a horde of sailors surging back and forth. To make things worse, the lights suddenly went out, spontaneously generating a yelling mob. It was like being in the path of a cattle stampede. We struggled to our feet and Fritz flicked on his Zippo and held it aloft. "Battle lanterns," he shouted. "Turn on the battle lanterns." In a few minutes the mob found the lanterns stashed about head-high at each watertight door and the panic stopped.

We resumed our slow, uphill progress to living quarters. The bomb blasts were further forward; so we found only smoke damage in the sleeping quarters. Where were the pilots?  On deck, we hoped. Simultaneously we thought of our men in the infirmary. With a growing sense of dread we made our way down the forward, running into more burned and walking wounded. As we got closer, we wondered why people like that were moving away from the infirmary?  In a single ghastly moment we stepped through a watertight door and found our answer. There was no infirmary. A heavy smell of cordite and licking flames told the story. One of the explosions we'd heard on the bridge had been this bomb. Stone and four others. Holy God. Blasted to hell. There was no use checking; the infirmary simply didn't exist.

Deeply depressed, we made our way back. By the time we reached the stateroom area the surging crowd had thinned. Martinez was home, sitting somewhat stunned on his bunk staring into space. He greeted us with open arms. "Commander!  Señor Mason!  Thank God."

Fritz and I embraced him and we continued our search. On impulse

I stopped at Stone's cabin although we'd already checked and found it to be empty. To our surprise my light tap on the door produced a familiar face. "You shit!" Fritz shouted, shaking his hand. "We thought you were dead!"

"Not yet, Commander," Stone said, struggling to his feet.

"What about those other guys?" he asked, reaching for his shirt.

I shook my head. "If they were there, they're gone. If they were back here—"

"Nobody's home" Fritz said. "Maybe they're on deck."

"I doubt it," Stone said. "Not one of 'em was what you'd call ambulatory." Stone did the best he could with his shirt. "Are we gonna sink, Commander?"

"Possibly," Fritz said. "You better get your ass topside."

"Okay. You fellas can take off. I'll make it."

My impulse was to stay and help him but he grabbed his pants aggressively and growled, "Git."

I looked at Fritz, who grinned and we "got."

Barry Barker, XO, was sweating in his firefighter's gear. So was I. How the hell did I get into this pickle? Quite simply; the kamikaze had put me out of work. The main deck was inoperative; there'd be no more planes taking off and landing for God knows how long so there'd be no briefing, no real ACI stuff to do. Yet the ship was suffering everywhere I looked. All very well to be an observer under normal circumstances when you're also doing your job. But the explosions had changed all that. You had to do whatever came to hand.

What came to hand was Barry, bleeding from cuts, smudged from fire, pouring with sweat. I was on the bridge when he came up reporting the difficulty of fighting the fire with so many dead. I had volunteered and now I was spraying foam on burning deck timbers and trying to reach the crew's quarters forward. The change of the ship's position relative to the wind to keep the smoke away from the bridges had put her bow directly into the seas, causing the familiar rise and fall, which I'd long since grown used to, but in the firefighting gear way up forward I felt uncomfortable. Having doused a barrier of flaming timbers, Barry stepped past them and turned into the crew's quarters. "Jesus," he said quietly. Stepping past him, I couldn't even say this much. The bomb blast had turned the off-duty crew into half-naked, dismembered bodies, some of whose clothing still lay scattered in smoking piles.

Wasn't war supposed to be the way the Victorian era portrayed it? Handsome men in bright uniforms saying fond farewells to loving sweethearts while the band played on? It was not supposed to carry the smell of roasted human flesh nor be seen in its raw brutality–a room of horror, twenty or thirty sailors, one minute a bunch of kids with ukuleles, radios, pin-ups, letters from home. The next minute victims of a scorching meat cleaver gone mad. I could feel my gorge rising, but having already seen what had happened on the hangar deck, I knew the solution; get busy.

"Nothing we can do here," Barker said brusquely. "Let's go."

We continued to search and snuff out sudden islands of flame, either eating at deck timbers or sizzling and popping along a painted bulkhead. Barry had a wonderful way of going from group to group, sharing their dangers, goading, praising, leading. I went along–more angry than anything else. It all seemed so senseless, so raw, ugly, unromantic. Some fool had changed the script. These were scenes nobody wanted to play. Good God, how could so much fire and smoke and screams and yells be anything but a bad dream? Would the ship even stay afloat? Why were so many people going overboard? Sliding down lines, leaping directly into the sea? Had the Captain announced, "abandon ship?" without my hearing it?

Fritz and I turned a corner and came upon a scene out of an old movie–filmed in bad lighting. We stepped into a passage right out of the Civil War, with wounded men lying on the deck on stretchers waiting to go into the operating room. Through the cracked glass panel I could see David Swartz in a bloody gown intent on his operation. A corpsman was rendering some assistance, handing instruments, wiping sweat from his face; another corpsman, looking pale and frightened, was apparently administering anesthetic. Where in hell were the other doctors? One look at the smoking hole that had been the forward half of the sick bay area and I knew the answer. Swartz, who wanted to save lives, now had his chance. How long had he been at it? How long could he stand there fighting to save these youngsters? As we watched, he finished whatever he was doing to the patient and stepped back while corpsmen lifted the man off the table and carried him out of sight into whatever was left of the hospital rooms. We could see David take a drink of water, wipe the sweat off his face with a piece of gauze, raise and lower his shoulders, and step forward as the corpsmen lifted another injured man on the table. I was amazed to see him bend over the new patient with a broad smile, and what must have been an encouraging word. Then the amateur anesthetist made an injection and covered the boy's face with a cone.

This was strictly medical–and out of our league. All we could do was send up a prayer that Swartz could hold out against so much injury, so many young men on the verge of death. Blinded by tears, I turned away and followed Fritz away from the horror.

# Twenty-six

I was on the bridge with McCord when a lookout saw the torpedo. The Captain quietly ordered the helmsman, "Hard right rudder." The big man at the wheel said, "Hard right rudder, sir," and swung the ship toward the incoming torpedo to reduce the target surface. McCord stepped out on the starboard wing to the bridge and picked up the line of bubbles with his glasses. He looked at the ship's angle of turn and shook his head; there would be an intercept. He ran inside and grabbed the microphone. At that moment the torpedo penetrated the hull below the waterline. Instead of exploding—we later learned—the projectile crossed the engine room and pierced the opposite bulkhead, blowing up outside the hull. The explosion, just below the bridge, knocked the Captain down, shattered glass, and knocked me flat. Getting to his feet, McCord looked at the helmsman and noticed that his face was bleeding. The windows of the wheelhouse had been broken and slivers of glass were everywhere. I brushed glass splinters off my shirt.

"Okay, Mike?"

I nodded.

"Keep her turning, Morgan. A second torpedo could be on the way."

"Aye, sir."

Crunching glass under foot, McCord stepped out on the wing of the bridge and searched for a second shot. No signs. Close aboard, a destroyer with klaxons screaming was turning at flank speed to find the sub. Smoke and flame poured up out of the huge chimney that had been the forward elevator. Two Hellcats that had been spotted forward were on fire. The bodies of a dozen sailors lay scattered across the deck. Along the wooden flight deck small lines of fire spurted, following the inset planking like small yellow flowers set in row.

The Captain returned to the pilothouse shaking his head. "Would you believe it? That fucking torpedo came out of the engine room twenty feet above the waterline. I wonder what happened."

He picked up the phone and tried to reach the engine room. Dead line. He slammed down the phone. "Goddamnit. I've got to learn what's going on down there. I want to know how much water we're taking."

He swung around in frustration and there I stood—Mercury without the winged foot—not exactly the perfect messenger but I'd have to do.

I wanted to yell, "Enough already." Wanted to scramble back to the flag bridge and busy myself with the Admiral's charts.     Instead, as the Captain turned to me asking the question with his eyebrows, I forced a grin and said, "Whatever you say, Captain."

"Go have a look," the Captain said. "Come back and tell me."

Cursing myself for a spineless idiot, I tried to find consolation by telling myself the ship was in mortal danger and everybody was giving his all.

I knew the way. It didn't involve another tough trip against the passageway. I slipped through a watertight door marked "Engine Room" and began my way down into the huge empty spaces of the engine room. Most of my descent was on steel catwalks, through which I could see the brightly lighted working areas. Strong smell of oil. Hum of small electric motors. Clang of wrenches. Shouts. Heat. Maybe 135-140 degrees. Within minutes my shirt was wet and sweat was rolling down my back. The catwalks seemed to go on forever. Below I saw huge boilers, big shiny electric motors, silent glistening engines and a group of half-naked men gathered around a small leader in shirt and pants. MacIver. Lieutenant Commander Sandy MacIver, an M.I.T. graduate, a quick wiry man with an easy grin. From above, it looked like a bright detail in a dark picture. Dutch school?  Mac seemed glad to see me. "Captain's having fits," I said. "Are we seaworthy or not?"

MacIver took off his steel-rimmed glasses and wiped them. He led me out of the lighted area into gloom, where I could hear the swish of water. Then I was wading in it as it sloshed back and forth. Then I saw the jury rig with the ocean squirting around it. Jury indeed?

Mac saw my expression and said, "Not bad really. Hell, you should have seen it before my men got to work. Before the pumps. We're damn lucky the torpedo struck the housing of the main shaft. Got deflected upwards and went out well above the waterline." Thus he answered the Captain's question. He pointed to a jagged hole through which I could see blue sky.

"How many men did you lose?" I asked.

"None!" he shouted proudly. "It didn't explode inside."

"Thank God. Can we stay afloat?"

"We can."

"So what do I tell the Captain?"

A hard Scottish glint came into his eyes. "Tell him she'll make it. Just send the mattresses on the double."

I climbed up the catwalks going fast, my heart pounding. By the time I reached the main bridge, I was badly out of breath but I managed to blurt out the good news.

"MacIver says she'll make it. The torpedo bounced off the main shaft housing and came out above the water line. No casualties. Send him mattresses on the double."

The Captain shook my hand in a hard grip then spoke into a microphone. "Captain calling XO. Captain calling XO.

A husky voice answers, "XO here."

"Brad, MacIver needs mattresses to plug a hole. Please get a damage control unit to the engine room on the double."

"Aye, sir. On the double."

I joined the group gathering around Terry Vernon and Fritz at the base of the island. At first glance my heart sank. Not more than half of the ninety-man group were there. Where were they? Fritz and I had checked the cabins and wardrooms. Forty or fifty men were still unaccounted for. Stone slowly emerged from below, carrying a life jacket and a picture in a wooden frame. He crossed over to us, ignoring the noise. Fritz stuck out his hand. Jesse shifted the picture and shook hands. When he had surveyed the chaos—firemen dragging hoses, sailors jumping and sliding down ropes—he asked, "Are we gonna lose her?"

I said "no" and told him about the engine room.

Stone pointed to the sailors jumping and sliding down lines into the water. "Somebody oughta tell those men. If we're not abandoning ship, they'll be in trouble." As though he had commanded us to do so, Fritz and I, followed by Terry, walked across the smoking deck and gathered around us as many would-be jumpers as possible. Each of us, addressing his group of sailors, said, "Don't jump. We're still seaworthy. There's been no 'abandon ship.'" There was some obedience, some panic; once a man has made up his mind to go over the side he's hard to deter.

We gave it up after a while and rejoined the fliers at the base of the island. Stone looked pale and sick. There was blood around the edge of his bandages. When I pointed to it he grimaced. "Too bad I haven't got that kid to take care of me." He put down the picture and slumped to the deck. I crouched beside him. "You okay?"

"Not exactly tiptop." He grinned at the use of an unfamiliar expression. I glanced at the picture. A thin woman in a plain house dress standing on the porch of a small wooden house. He tapped the glass. "The old lady." I could hardly hear him in the midst of the yelling, intermittent explosions, and wind gusts. "My mother. Miner's wife. I was just a kid when the old man was killed. Sixteen men with him. Explosion and fire. She stood at the pit head twenty-four hours waiting for news."

He wrapped the picture in the life jacket and lay back against the island structure, calm and fatalistic.

Fritz did a quick new headcount and asked me if I'd go below to see if we'd missed anybody. "Look in the heads, the wardroom, the cabins. Christ, wherever they might have gone."

Having already been below in those crowded smoky passages, I wasn't too anxious to comply, but if Fritz needed a final check on his people, how could I refuse? Once again, I plunged into the crowd and once again did my salmon-upstream act, running into the usual panic-stricken kids scrambling to reach the open air, intermixed with more mature types—most of them chiefs—who were bound for a battle station or in rare instances—were trying to save their skin, like the youngsters.

After some difficulty and much verbal abuse—"Where the fucking hell do you think you're going?"—I managed to reach our eating-and-sleeping area and found a dozen fliers in the wardroom; they'd plugged the doors with wet dinner napkins. I chased them topside—"Commander Rawlings wants you on deck—base of the island. Pronto."

I went from room to room, finding no one, until I reached Martinez' cubicle. To my amazement he was lying on his bunk, half-dressed. His eyes were closed and his lips were moving as if in prayer. I shook him and he sat up, exclaiming, "Sorry, sir."

"Rawlings wants everybody topside."

"Are we sinking? *Madre de Dios.*"

"I dunno."

He swung his feet to the deck.

"Get dressed," I said sharply. "Let's move it."

He obeyed. Before we left the cubicle, I wasn't surprised to see him remove the crucifix and rosary.

"Stay close," I said, as we stepped into the smoking passageway. I broke a path for him, sometimes at the expense of good manners. "Move it, sailor. You're blocking the fucking line!" Sometimes caught up in the emotional urge to get out of there and reach the open air, I told myself I was doing it for Marty; in truth, like everyone else, I was yielding to a desperate personal desire to get out of the smoke and reach the open air.

Once I got Martinez to the base of the island I knew I'd had it with missions below deck. I looked around and the confidence I brought back from the engine room began to fade. The view facing forward was not encouraging. The explosions had broken a great hole near the bow. Twisted beams reaching upward told me there'd be no more take-offs from this flight deck. Smoke and flames were still coming out of the forward elevator shaft. Our forward motion had ceased and we were drifting sideways with the wind.

As I reached the bridge the Captain asked, "What's the pilot count?"

"Maybe thirty missing sir," I said. "I just found a dozen in the wardroom."

He said, "I imagine the Admiral will be leaving. He can't run this operation from *Sussex*. We've got too many broken communications."

I went down the ladder two at a time and found the old man studying his charts and listening to the Chief of Staff's briefing. It was as if his headquarters—our beleaguered ship—were sailing serenely on course with not a cloud in the sky. He turned as he heard me enter and studied me over his glasses, smiling, until he spoke.

"What've you been up to, Mason? You're a mess." He seemed amused.

I'd forgotten where I'd been.

Deciding to ignore the question, I found a hip-pocket handkerchief and wiped my face. He became instantly serious. "Losses?"

"We're not sure, sir. Captain thinks at least eight hundred."

"Goddamn! One rotten little Jap kills almost a third of our people! Are we seaworthy?"

"For the moment, yes. The torpedo only made one waterline hole."

"I guess I'll have to move." He said this with regret.

"We'd be sorry to have you go, sir."

"That makes me a rat, doesn't it? Deserting a sinking ship." We both grinned.

"Captain said you needed communications and we've lost 'em."

"Right. An operation like this is Communication with a big C."

Were we talking like this on a ship that was fighting fires, taking in water, counting the dead, trying to deal with the wounded? I found it unreal. Yet a single glance told me that this was no place for headquarters. The old man's coolness in the face of it all made me ashamed of any desperation in the passageways. Was this the difference between an amateur and the pros? I was grateful that none of them was a mind reader.

I listened as Stowell brought him reports of other kamikaze attacks, and he accepted them as if they had been part of the original invasion plan. When he heard that the Marines were ashore in five places, he nodded in satisfaction as if he were visualizing waves of men coming out of the landing craft and charging up the steep beaches to the temporary safety of thick palms as the beachhead took shape.

The Admiral spotted the second enemy plane before the alarm sounded. He touched my elbow and pointed.

Stowell removed his pipe and said, "Here we go again." The P.A. blared, "Bogey starboard side, bogey starboard side. Commence firing."

As I watched the plane with the meatball on its wings, I had a split-second memory flash of walking through a field out of season and seeing a big pheasant flying overhead. How I had yearned for a gun, now, with the big bird overhead. At this point a *Sussex* shell struck the plane and it exploded within 50 yards of the ship.

"Nice shot," the Admiral muttered. I felt as if I'd done it myself.

# Twenty-seven

As the third kamikaze came screaming down the pilots who were huddled around the island scattered like chickens jumped by a fox. Just for a heartbeat the sight of the enemy plane nailed me to the spot. Terror gripped me as I watched machine gun rounds gouging up teak splinters in my direction. I ran for the tub where the anti-aircraft gun was pumping shells into the sky in alternating bursts. In the split second before I snatched off my glasses to save them, my eyes caught sight of Fritz on the run. Some trace of high school geometry told me that the path of the marching bullets would converge with Fritz. No!

The metal plane then struck the metal island in a shrieking collision that drove ice picks into my ears; followed by an explosion which must have told the young kamikaze pilot that the road to the Emperor's garden began in hell's half-acre.

Deafened and stunned, but free of wounds, I slowly stood up and looked back where I'd stood with the fliers. Bodies lay everywhere, as men ran towards the island pulling hoses.

When I found Fritz he was dead. The round had entered the back of his head and burst out of his face. I couldn't look a second time. As I stood up, fighting nausea, Stone approached. He saw my expression and bent over Fritz. It seemed quite a while before he straightened up. He had to lean close to be heard. "Sorry, Mike."

I wanted to say something cool and casual in the fliers' tradition— "You win some; you lose some"—but my voice shut down. A weak "Yeah" was all that came out. I cleared my throat. "Gotta check the bridges."

As I turned away there stood Terry looking past me at Fritz. Slowly he put a hand on my shoulder. Neither of us spoke. I finally turned away and went up to the bridge.

As I arrived the Captain was wiping blood from his face with a towel. He shouted to be heard above the roar of the burning plane. "Mike, you made it."

"Fritz Rawlings is dead," I managed to say.

He grimaced and shook his head. "Goddamn shame. How's the old man?"

"On my way down there now."

I managed to pick my way through the chaos to the ladder and went down to flag bridge. I found the Admiral lying on the deck with three staff officers bending over him. What *next?* Captain Stowell was saying, "He's coming around. Give him some air. How do you feel, sir?"

There was a mumbled response. Then the old man raised himself on one elbow, cleared his throat, and asked hoarsely, "How's the Captain. Tell me about McCord."

I took this as my cue and climbed up the ladder to the main bridge. The Captain was issuing orders to the OD. The broad glass facade of the bridge had already been partially shattered; now it was gone, admitting the noise of the flight deck -- the roar and crackle of the burning flames, the shouts of the firefighters, the rattle of gunfire as ammo exploded on the hangar deck. The Captain's arm was bleeding.

"The Admiral wants to know how you are?" I shouted.

"Okay," he yelled. "What about him?"

"Knocked down. Don't know the damage."

"We'll have to get him off this ship."

"Aye, sir."

The heavy cruiser *Birmingham*, having observed the kamikaze strike, was heading our way. She would be the obvious new headquarters of Task Force 68, since, I assumed, *Sussex* was no longer fully functional as a communications center. As I listened, the Captain officially sent out the call, bringing *Birmingham* closer. The huge grey cruiser, big as a battleship in my eyes, with enough guns to take on half the Japanese Navy, moved swiftly toward us, white water at her prow.

The XO and his asbestos-suited fire crew began to make headway on the fire. As the smoke started to clear I saw the corpsman checking bodies scattered around the foot of the island, where the Japanese bombs had torn the jagged hole. I counted seven young fliers, who only the day before had stood so proudly almost on the same spot to accept their Distinguished Flying Crosses. Choked with emotion, I returned to flag bridge to do anything I could to help the Admiral transfer his headquarters. He was on his feet now with a left arm that he seemed to be favoring. His face was bloody from a cut above the eye.

"Captain McCord sends his respects, sir. He's okay."

"Thanks. What about casualties?"

I had a hard time answering. "Fritz Rawlings, sir, and at least seven other fliers."

"Fritz?" he said. "Damn."

All I could do was nod.

"And the little fellow who won the Navy Cross?"

"He's okay."

"Good."

He wiped his face with a handkerchief.

"I guess I'll have to move."

"Sorry, sir."

"You better stay with the group."

"Aye, sir."

"McCord's getting me a ship?"

"Yes, sir. *Birmingham's* closing."

I pointed. The great gray presence of the heavy cruiser *Birmingham* was growing larger by the minute as she surged toward us. She was the ultimate warship; I was glad her mission was not aggressive toward the drifting floating island of dead and wounded that our ship had become. After her high-speed approach, she spun in a tight turn and skillfully maneuvered herself alongside to receive the Admiral. She chose upwind to escape the smoke and flames. She let the wind push her alongside and give us a gentle bump. Immediately, her people scrambled across with fire hoses. The XO, with a working bullhorn, supervised the crossing and directed the new firefighters. A feeling of hope came with her; the Navy helping the Navy.

A line was shot across from the bridge and fastened at our end. Captain McCord, looking very much unlike himself in torn trousers, ripped shirt and bloody face, came down to escort the Admiral. For a moment they faced each other in silence, though the windowless flag bridge was hardly silent, filled with the roar of fire, the shouts of the XO's, crew, plus the thump of explosions below on the hangar deck.

The Captain said, "Sorry to have you leave, sir."

The Admiral put his hand on the shorter man's shoulder. "Sorry to go, Jim. What's your condition?"

The Captain said, "We'll make it, sir. They tell me she's seaworthy."

The Admiral managed a smile. "Good luck, Jim. Get her plugged up and sail her home."

"Aye, sir."

They shook hands and the Captain walked the Admiral to the point of transfer, helped him into the gear he had to wear as they swung him over the high line. Halfway across the Admiral turned and waved; from a hundred throats came a mighty cheer as the cruiser crew pulled him to safety.

I watched the old man with deep emotion, torn between a desire to be with him and a realization that *Sussex* was in trouble, the CAG was dead, many young fliers were dead and the Air Group was shattered.

Once the Admiral and Stowell were aboard, *Birmingham* withdrew her lines, reversed her engines and eased away from us. Her great gray presence had been a momentary comfort. As she pulled away we seemed suddenly alone. I returned to the main bridge as the Captain finished a conversation. "Finally got through to Mac. He says the pumps are gaining. Water's stopped coming in. He's got good boiler pressure and the engines are turning."

"Great."

The fire seemed to be doused at the base of the island, though bitter wisps of smoke still rose from the jagged hole in the deck.

I realized that Air Group One Thirteen would be getting R and R in Pearl, then probably return stateside for either refitting or demobilization depending on the state of the war. Either alternative would not involve me. A new CAG would select his own ACI. The chicanery that got me the job should be able to reverse itself. Surely a Navy that had accepted me so reluctantly would welcome my departure. I was ready.

The Captain walked to the outer wing of the bridge with a bullhorn. Looking down at the men in the water, he began to talk to the destroyer which was gathering them up in cargo nets. "Ahoy, below. This is McCord. Pick up all the people you can find and stand by to follow us. Thanks for your help." From the destroyer came an answering bullhorn. "Aye, sir. We'll fish 'em out."

McCord went back inside the shattered bridge and to the mike. "Now hear this. Captain speaking. We are still at General Quarters. This ship has *not* secured from General Quarters. We can't launch or land planes, but we can still shoot and we can still fight fires. We are not abandoning ship. Repeat. Not abandoning ship. We have taken two kamikaze hits, but we are seaworthy. We have power. If you have left your battle station, get the hell back there at once."

A frantic procession had begun to form in the passageways where there had been a concerted rush to reach the flight deck and open air. The Captain's words brought this procession to a halt. They changed direction, slowly thinned out, started back to guns and water hoses.

The Admiral was on the radio from *Birmingham*. "How goes it, McCord?"

"Still afloat, sir. Seaworthy."

"Casualties?"

McCord found it hard to answer. "Eight hundred to one thousand, sir."

"You better pull out, Mac. I meant what I said. Take 'em to Ulithi and home."

"Aye, sir."

McCord was dead tired, but there was a pride in his voice. Again he was holding a mike and talking to his crew. "This is the Captain. We have the latest damage control reports. We've got the hole patched below our waterline, and we've got the main fires out. If you thought we were going to sink, you were wrong. This ship is going to make it." He paused and the quality of his voice changed. "We have lost a lot of people. The count isn't exact, but it's more than eight hundred men." Another pause. "Our Air Group is scattered all over hell, but they'll find us." He took a deep breath. "This ship has been relieved of its position in the line. We are going home. First stop: Ulithi, then Pearl. Thank you for everything you have done. Carry on."

Climbing slowly towards the bridge, I reached the charred flight deck in the midst of a crowd of the pilots at the base of the island. We listened to the Captain, looking up at the bridge where the voice came from. Where was the rest of the Air Group?

Without the sound of aircraft taking off or landing, the great blackened ship was strangely quiet.

# Twenty-eight

*The young white crane*
*innocently sets his course*
*above the waiting hunter's gun.*

The Army kamikaze group was finally flexing its muscle. The huge U.S. fleet was coming in range and propellers were whirling. Niki Osaka, a careful planner, was ready for his venture. He went through the motions of farewell. He bowed to the hated Colonel. He double-checked every aspect of his plane. And he smiled as he listened to the weather report: Low clouds and rain. Just what he needed. The Colonel might have been curious that a young man on his way to a suicide dive should need two canteens of water and two sandwiches; very curious. He might also have wondered why the young flier needed a surface chart of the home islands when his targets were in the Philippines, and a parachute! He'd hidden that aboard his plane at night.

Niki took off third and formed up beside his fellows. For five minutes he appeared to be exactly like all the other eager suiciders with whom he was exchanging salutes, waves and thumbs-up gestures. Up ahead he saw what he was looking for: A broad cloud bank that the group would have to penetrate. Just as they entered the cloud Niki deliberately switched his motor off and on, giving the audible impression of engine trouble. He repeated the move, then dove away to the right and headed northwest. He was happy to see that the cloud formation was coming from that direction, covering his escape. When he broke out of the overcast, he found himself directly above an American escort carrier and two destroyers. His first impulse was to get back in the cloud bank. Then all three ships exploded with gunfire, the carrier and the two destroyers sending up black flowers that seemed to be exploding all over the sky.

One detonated so close he could feel its strong thrust tipping his wing. The next one burst close aboard, shattering his cowling. Immediately, the cockpit began to fill with smoke.

Niki felt a mounting fury. This was not in his plan. He didn't want to be mixed up in all this gunfire. These fools didn't understand that he meant them no harm. Now they'd set his plane on fire. Idiots! He craned his neck and saw flames spurting from the tail section. That did it. With sudden resolve he pushed hard on his right rudder and swung the Zero around. Holding his breath, he pushed the stick forward in an act of reflexive anger. He plunged straight down, with the wind screaming through the open cockpit. As the American ship grew larger, Niki had a change of heart. He pushed hard with his feet and made a sharp turn to the right. At the diving speed he'd reached he quickly found the shelter of a low lying cloud. He climbed again, now hidden from the carrier, and bailed out of the burning plane over land. As he drifted down he watched his plane hit the ground and explode. Gently, feeling wildly happy and excited, he floated to earth, touching down in a rice paddy. Two elderly women ran to him chattering in Japanese. He smiled, feeling he'd make it home after all.

Kei was standing on her terrace, holding her husband's letter. She had lived this moment many times in her mind. Now the threat was no longer a threat. *Amato* was gone. The letter said it was going to happen. The harsh headlines of the newspaper said it had happened.

Kei was angry. Angry at the Japanese Navy for sending *Amato* to be sacrificed. Angry at her husband for obeying such foolish orders. Most of all she was angry at the Americans whose planes had destroyed her husband's great ship.

Where were the boys? Where was Ken? Where was Niki? Where was Miro? Were they alive? The grocer's son had said Niki had a plan. The wind snatched her husband's letter and blew it against a peony bush, where she retrieved it. The ink had begun to run. Kei went inside and a servant brought a towel and dried her face. Hot tea took away the chill. She folded the letter and put it back in the envelope. Then she picked up the newspaper and began to reread the story of *Amato's* destruction.

# Twenty-nine

I was on my way home at last. What had I proved in the months I'd been at sea? Standing with Terry Vernon, Ben Nevitt, and the XO amid the smoking ruin of the hangar deck, I shuddered at the recollections of what had happened there. I wondered if they too had felt the deep and paralyzing fear that had gripped me? Nevitt maybe. But not the XO; he was too busy; he was a pro. I thought of all the times I had briefed the young pilots, cool and casual as I warned them about the presence of anti-aircraft defenses, vicariously flying with them, and later recording their boyish tales of diving into gunfire, striking targets, occasionally losing a comrade. Death was remote from me; now it had stared me in the face and I knew that I was no hero. I was just a half-blind Virginia graduate who had shared in great events without shaping them and—as Maggie said—it was high time I went home and behaved like a husband and father.

We could smell land before dawn on the easterly wind. For many days we had lived aboard a ship that smelled of smoke, burnt paint, gasoline and cordite. The aroma of Hawaii seemed a delicious change. Was it the pineapples growing? Was it all those flowering trees? Was it the orange-blossom leis?

Few of us slept that last night. I had played chess with the Captain and actually won. Had he let me have his queen in a sentimental moment? Those not assigned to duty were on deck before sun up. We talked in little quiet groups—fliers, sailors, officers. For the moment there was no naval structure as each man spoke of going ashore, getting liberty, calling home.

As daybreak came, the ship's routines resumed. Orders were cut, food was cooked, coffee perked, shoes polished, whites pressed, trombones brassed. Landfall was scheduled at zero-six-hundred, liberty beginning at ten-hundred. Daylight brought us the tops of the submerged mountain chain, looking somewhat like the back of a huge monster. Then the green islands rose from the sea and with them our spirits lifted. We'd made it. Our great beat-up ship had brought us home. By this time we could identify Diamond Head. Two big Navy tugs were chugging out to meet us. At this point they were more ceremonial than useful. The Captain standing on a battered wing of the bridge was pressed and dapper, ready for inspection.

As we passed Diamond Head the XO turned out the sailors in a rectangle from the island aft—a phalanx of brown-faced young men in white standing at ease as the band, in the center, played "Anchors Aweigh." I wouldn't say this was the finest rendition of the great old song I'd ever heard, but it didn't matter since the tugs began hooting and every ship in the harbor seemed to be joining in a noisy salute. As usual, I had some trouble seeing; but this time it had nothing to do with those specs.